"I DON'T WANT things to be different," says Ali Rose about leaving her mother and New York to spend the summer with her father and his new wife in California, where they used to live. For Ali, returning to California turns out to be a series of unexpected changes.

Open and naive, Ali has always tried to please everyone. But she is soon faced with situations that force her to realize that her indecisiveness could cost her the things that mean the most. When she falls in love with her best friend Gretchen's brother, Ali has so many conflicts about Gretchen's insecurities where her brother is concerned that she keeps the relationship a secret. But then she is caught in the middle—faced with losing one of the people she most cares about.

Perhaps even more upsetting are her father's implications that her mother's friendship with a woman named Peggy goes further than friendship—implications she refuses to accept. But when things come to a head, Ali finds herself caught between parents with contrasting values and lifestyles, who both want her enough to fight for her. Shuttled emotionally between them, Ali realizes that she can't allow others to make her decisions; she must make her own.

In this warm and compelling story, Norma Klein once again accurately portrays family life with all its tensions and strengths. What emerges are real people who are tested many times before they fully recognize the price and value of love and commitment.

Breaking Up

a novel by

NORMA KLEIN

Pantheon Books

Published in the United States by Pantheon Books,
A Division of Random House, Inc. and simultaneously in Canada
by Random House of Canada Limited, Toronto.
Library of Congress Cataloging in Publication Data
Klein, Norma, 1938–
Breaking Up.
SUMMARY: While she is visiting her father and stepmother
in California, 15-year-old Alison learns her mother is a lesbian.
[1. Divorce—Fiction. 2. Remarriage—Fiction.
3. Lesbians—Fiction] I. Title.
PZ7.K678345Lo 1980 [Fic] 80–10953
ISBN 0–394–84445–9   ISBN 0–394–94445–3 lib. bdg.
Manufactured in the United States of America
3 5 7 9 10 8 6 4 2

TO MY MOTHER

Breaking Up

One

"Okay, now listen," Mom said. "We have half an hour to think."

"About what?" Peggy asked.

"Everything we may have forgotten," said Mom.

Peggy looked at me, smiled, and said to Mom, "Come on, Cindy, nothing's been forgotten."

"There's always some tiny but crucial thing that you don't think of till you're on the plane," Mom said. "Look, Ali," she said to me, "go in your room and sit there for five minutes and *think*, really think."

I stood up and sighed.

"Was she always this obsessive?" Peggy asked good-naturedly.

"Yeah," my brother Martin said.

"Mothers are like that," I said.

"It's a little gene," Martin said, "that fizzles up as soon as a kid is born. It happens to all of them."

"I'll have to take your word for it," said Peggy.

Peggy doesn't have any kids. She said she never had the time. One night we had a talk about it. She married young, like Mom, but got divorced a year later. She said the guy was someone who was really a good friend. "He was fine as a *friend*," she said. "We should have left it that way." Peggy said she could imagine herself adopting a teenager, but not going through the whole "diaper bit" as she put it. I'm glad Mom got friendly with her. She's a very calm, down-to-earth person with a good sense of humor. She never seems to get rattled the way Mom often does.

I went into my room and sat there, trying to think if there was anything I'd forgotten. I was sure I had everything. It just seems amazing that it's finally happening, that Martin and I are actually going back to California. We lived there all our lives, even after Mom and Daddy got divorced seven years ago. Then last year, Mom was offered this really good job at the Metropolitan Museum—she's a curator of ancient instruments—and we had to move three thousand miles across the country, away from school, all our friends, everything! When we first came to New York, I really *hated* it. It wasn't New York so much, though it did seem dirty and cold and unfriendly after Berkeley. It was more missing everything. In Berkeley I have a really good friend, Gretchen, who's been my best, *best* friend for years. Now that I've been in New York a year I have *some* friends, but no one I feel really close to, the way I do to Gretchen. I guess you just don't make close friends that easily—at least not the kind you can talk to about everything and know they'll understand.

I feel excited about going back for the summer, but

not as excited as I thought I'd be. It all seems so far away. I wrote to Gretchen over the winter a little, but I'm not such a good letter writer and neither is she. Now I wonder if we'd still be able to talk the way we used to. And I wonder a little about Teddy, too. He's this boy I used to go with in junior high. I guess he was sort of in love with me. I wasn't in love with him though, which was a problem. I mean, I *liked* him a lot. He's a really nice person and good-looking and all of that. But I never felt the way I think you're supposed to feel when you're in love with somebody.

Peggy looked in. "Any last-minute inspirations?"

I shook my head.

"Anyhow, if you do leave something behind, we can just send it to you," she said.

I walked out into the hall and looked into Martin's room. "Aren't you going to take your typewriter?" I asked, seeing it on his desk.

He shook his head. "I don't think I'll need it especially."

Every time I see Martin's typewriter I feel guilty because of something I did a while ago. It happened one day when I was typing in his room. Mom got Martin this really great typewriter for his seventeenth birthday. You can switch the ribbon to any color—green, blue, red— depending on what mood you're in. I like that idea. Once in a while Martin lets me use it, but I'm supposed to ask his permission each time, which really bugs me. This time he was out and I wanted to write a letter to Gretchen. I opened one of his drawers and started looking for typing paper since there wasn't any on the desk. Just as I opened it, this sheet of paper, which had been folded up, kind of jumped right into my hand. I'm not kidding; it really did. I started to put it back, but then I just happened to see a couple of lines, and before I knew it I'd read the whole thing! I could tell it was from Tess, Martin's girl friend, by the handwriting. The thing is, it was this really sexy letter, telling about all these things they used to do together and that she was wishing they could be doing now. I never knew they did *any* of those things!

Maybe it's because he's my brother, but I just can't imagine Martin even *kissing* anybody, much less the rest of it. I know he's good-looking. He's tall, over six feet, and he has a good build, but he's always scowling. He's a very moody person, Mom says, always way up or way down in terms of how he feels. He and Tess met because they were both on the tennis team at school. She's little and spry and has freckles and short, curly brown hair. I guess you'd call her cute, but not that sexy-looking or acting. I always thought they just kind of played tennis and went on picnics and stuff, whereas it turns out they used to go someplace in the Berkeley hills behind the tennis courts and take their clothes off under a blanket and do just about *everything!* It was *really* an interesting letter, but I know it was wrong of me to read it. Martin would *kill* me if he found out. I put it back very neatly so he'd never know.

While I was thinking about all this, Mom came into

the room. "Why don't we start out?" she said. "It always pays to be a little early."

"I'm going to miss you, Ali Cat," Mom said after our bags had been checked through. Ali Cat's a nickname she had for me when I was little.

"Me too," I said. I suddenly felt like I might cry.

"Call me if you feel like talking, at work or home, any time."

I nodded.

Mom smiled. "You'll have a terrific time, Ali, seeing Gretchen and Teddy again, all your friends."

"Yeah." I tried to look cheerful.

"The first week will be hard, but after that you'll forget you ever left."

"Mom, come on. We better get moving," Martin said.

"See you in a couple of months," Peggy said, hugging me. I hugged her back. "Don't worry, I'll take care of her," she said, putting her hand on Mom's shoulder.

"Give my love to Tess," Mom said, looking up at Martin.

He bent down and kissed her. "I will," he said. "Take it easy, Mom."

It was the kind of plane where you walk right on and don't have to go outside. Martin went ahead of me and found our seats. I sat down on the middle one.

"Don't you want the window?" he asked.

"No, you take it. Maybe we can switch later." I don't

mind flying. I even enjoy it, but I never like that feeling when the plane's taking off. Once you're up in the air and can't see anything except clouds and stuff, it's not so bad. It's hard to imagine the plane crashing when you can't see anything for it to crash into.

"Marty, who paid for the tickets?" I asked after a minute. "Mom or Daddy?"

"How should *I* know?"

"I think it was Daddy," I said. "Well, he should. He makes more money."

"That's not how it works. The whole thing is worked out by lawyers way ahead of time."

"Even things like that?"

"Everything."

"But how do they know what's going to come up?"

"Look, Ali, these people aren't lamebrains. It's their profession to figure out what will come up. Obviously, if parents live three thousand miles apart, someone's going to have to pay for transportation."

I thought for a moment. "Do you wish we still lived there, in Berkeley?"

"Yeah."

"I guess basically I do too," I said hesitantly. "But I've gotten used to New York a little." I glanced over at him. "I guess you miss Tess a lot, don't you?"

Martin grunted in his noncommunicative way and began staring out the window again with the sort of self-absorbed look he always gets when I bring up anything personal. I'd be insulted, except I have the feeling Martin is like Daddy that way—he doesn't like to talk about personal things. I'm just the opposite—I like to talk about personal things all the time! Gretchen does too.

I hope it'll be okay living with Eileen and Daddy for the summer. They've been married five years—since I was ten. Mom says Eileen takes being a stepmother very seriously. I think that's true. In her study she has all these books with titles like *How to Get Along with Your Husband's Children* or *Second Wife: Blessing or Curse?* She must have a dozen books like that! Once I looked through one of them, and she even had parts underlined with little exclamation points next to them. One thing she'd put a mark next to said something like: "Do not be surprised if at first your teenage stepson acts unusually cool toward you. He may be fighting off a strong sexual attraction, and his coolness may be a way of hiding his feelings, even from himself." That kind of cracked me up. It's hard to imagine Martin having a great undiscovered passion for Eileen. Another underlined part said: "Try and plan little outings together with your stepdaughter. Remember though—do not overstep the bounds. Let her call you whatever is most comfortable. Do not insist on her calling you Mom." I'd *never* call Eileen "Mom"!

"Is this 36C?" a man asked, pointing to the aisle seat next to me. He was short and plump with grayish-brown hair and glasses.

"I think so," I said, looking at the numbers above the seats.

"Good . . . I'll just set down my things then."

I saw him glance over at Martin, who was still gazing

intently out the window. Sometimes when Martin and I are together, people think he's my boyfriend. Martin's only two years older than me, but since he's gotten so tall, a lot of people assume he's in college. Whenever anyone thinks I'm his girlfriend, Martin gets furious. I guess he thinks it's an insult that someone would think he was so hard up he'd pick *me* for a girlfriend. Not that I'd want *him* for a boyfriend either, even if he wasn't my brother. I never could figure out why Tess likes him so much. She's really cute; you figure she could have a choice. Still, I suppose Martin's different with her than he is with me. With me he's always so condescending, as if he were about ten years older and as if everything I say is so dumb. I mean, it's true, I'm not intellectual the way he is, but that doesn't make me dumb either.

"Pardon me, would you care for a drink?" the stewardess asked.

"I'll have a daiquiri," I said.

Martin glared at me. "Oh come on, Ali. Don't show off."

"I'm *not!* I like them."

I know I look older when I wear makeup. Usually I don't wear any or maybe just lip gloss, but last month I went to Bloomingdale's in New York with this friend of mine, Hannah, and they did a free makeup demonstration on me. They put on eye shadow and all that stuff, and I looked at least eighteen! So now if I'm going somewhere special, I try to make myself up the way the woman in the store did.

"I'll have a Coke," Martin said.

"Why don't I bring you two Cokes?" the stewardess said, smiling at us.

"Make it three," the man next to me said. "Say, where are you and your boyfriend going?"

"He's *not* my boyfriend," I said, glaring at Martin. "He's my brother. And we're going to Berkeley to stay with my father and stepmother. Our parents are divorced. They always used to live in the same place; but last year Mom got this job in New York, and we had to move."

"That's always traumatic," the man said. "I don't see *my* daughter as often as I'd like, either. She lives with her mother, too. In fact, I haven't seen her in months. Luckily, I have a business that brings me near San Francisco."

"How old is she?" I asked.

"She's about your age, sixteen," he said. He cleared his throat. "She's a wonderful person."

"Do you have any pictures of her?" I love to look at photos of people.

His face lit up. "Yes, as a matter of fact I do. These are from last year." He took a few color snapshots out of his pocket. One was of a girl riding a horse. "She's crazy about horses," he said fondly.

"She looks nice," I said, giving the photos back to him.

"I really miss her a lot," he said. "Well, I'm sure your father feels the same way about you."

"I guess . . . I don't know." I wonder if Daddy would show people my picture on planes and say I was a wonderful girl.

"By the way," the man said. "My name's Sam Peterson. You're—?"

"Ali," I said. "Alison Rose."

He smiled. "People must make a lot of comments to you about your name, so I'll forbear."

I blushed. Actually, they do.

"Blooming and all that," he said.

"Yeah, well, you get used to it." I looked up at him. "Did *you* get married again? Daddy did. He married this woman named Eileen."

"Yes, I did," Mr. Peterson said.

"Do you have any pictures of your wife?"

"No, I don't. I'm sorry."

I guess people don't carry pictures of their wives as much as of their children. "Are you *happily* married?"

He laughed. "Well, yes, I think so . . . as these things go. Is your father?"

I thought a minute. "I guess. They don't scream at each other or anything, but they don't go around kissing every second either."

"Is that your definition of happiness?" he asked.

I blushed again. I have this terrible habit of blushing, especially when I say something dumb. "I suppose people do that more when they're young," I said.

"I suppose." He kept smiling at me.

Then something awful happened. I had two magazines on my lap, and they slipped to the floor. Mr.

Peterson picked them up and glanced at the covers. They were two magazines I'd bought before we got on the airplane: *Seventeen* and *Playgirl*. I always buy *Seventeen* when I buy *Playgirl*, because I'd feel sleazy just buying *Playgirl*. Or I buy gum or Lifesavers or something to make it look like I just *happened* to be buying *Playgirl*, maybe for my mother or something.

Every time Martin sees me looking at the centerfolds in *Playgirl* he says something sarcastic like, "Are you going to pin them up on your wall?" Mom says to ignore him. She says it's perfectly healthy and normal for a girl my age to be interested in what men look like without their clothes. I've read a lot of books where a girl sees a guy naked for the first time and she's really shocked at how he looks. I wouldn't want that happening to me. The ones I *don't* like are the men who have these sort of leering expressions and lots of curly hair and big white teeth. They look dumb. I like the more sensitive-looking ones who are studying physics or music or something artistic. Martin says they just make that part up, just like they always say the Playmate of the Month in *Playboy* is getting her master's degree in sociology. But it *could* be true; you can't tell. I also like it when they're shown doing something natural, like having a cup of coffee, not stretched out on a fur rug. The fur-rug types look like they know they're handsome. I bet if you met them, they'd be conceited.

One thing I don't understand is how these men let their real names be used. That would be the most embarrassing part. Imagine going on a date with someone, a blind date, and you'd ask what his name was and he'd say "Bob Smith," and you'd remember you'd seen him naked before you even met him!

Mom says there's one danger to my looking at these pictures. She says I might assume *all* men are gorgeous and have tiny waists and huge muscles. She says I should remember there are lots of very nice men who have potbellies and skinny legs. I *do* know that. I've seen lots of regular men on the beach, and I know how they look.

Mr. Peterson leafed through the magazine before handing it back to me. "It's a new phenomenon, I suppose," he said.

"What?"

"Oh, girls like you or Barbara buying magazines like this. I suppose it's a healthy thing."

"Well, I don't buy it *that* often," I said hastily, "just sometimes. . . . They have good articles," I added and blushed again. That was the third time I'd blushed in about half an hour!

"Rose in bloom," he said pensively, looking at me.

For the rest of the trip I watched the movie. It wasn't that good. Martin likes to watch without earphones. He says that way he can supply his own dialogue. Mr. Peterson started watching, but he fell asleep in the middle.

When we started to descend, he woke up.

"It wasn't that good," I told him.

"Did the good guys win?"

"Yeah, pretty much."

He sat forward and began getting his things together. "Say, Alison? I was wondering. . . . I might be back in this area in a month or so, and I thought—I think you and my daughter Barbara would really get along. Could I call you? Perhaps the three of us could go out some evening—bowling or to a movie or whatever?"

"Oh, sure," I said. I wrote down Eileen and Daddy's number. "That would be nice."

"I enjoyed talking to you," he said. "I hope you have a good stay with your father and stepmother."

"Me too." I could see Martin giving me a funny glance, but I decided to ignore him. It's always best to ignore Martin. He can make you feel really awful even if you haven't done anything wrong.

Two

"Well, I guess you told him our whole life story," Martin said as we were getting our bags.

"I didn't!" I said. "Anyway, what else is there to do on a plane except talk and think about things?"

"That last part doesn't come easily to all of us," he said sarcastically.

"What's wrong? Couldn't you think while we were talking?" Sometimes Martin gets me so *mad!*

"It *was* a little tricky," he said. "Luckily, being endowed with extraordinary powers of concentration, I managed."

"Poor you," I said. I'm not usually sarcastic, but Martin brings it out in me.

"How do you know he was even interested? You grab this poor guy and give him all the details of your life without even—"

"He *was* interested," I said, hurt.

"Sure. How come you gave him our phone number?"

"Well, he has this daughter my age, Barbara, and he said—"

"Sure."

"Marty, would you quit saying 'Sure' about everything? Don't you think he *has* a daughter, or what?"

"He probably has a thing for young girls or something."

"Come *on!* He was around forty!"

"So?"

"You're really sexist, you know that?" I said. "Can't somebody even *talk* to me without it being for some seedy reason?"

"Rose in bloom?" he said, teasing me now.

"He just had a poetic personality. Marty, will you stop looking at me that way?"

"How am I looking at you?"

"*You* know."

"Did you show him all your favorite playmates of the month?"

"He said he thought it was a very healthy phenomenon, looking at pictures like that. Not everybody has a dirty mind like you. Anyway, how come you were listening to every word we said?"

"Only every other word."

Eileen picked us up at the airport. At first we didn't see her because she had parked right outside where the taxis were. But when she saw us coming, she let out a yell. "Sorry I couldn't get out," she said, "but they wouldn't let me park. Hop in."

Eileen is tall, around five-foot-nine, and lanky. She has streaked blond hair, which is shiny and straight; she wears her sunglasses pushed back. One of the things you notice about her is that she has very straight white teeth, like she really brushed them the way dentists say you should. I guess she could be sexy, but her personality is sort of serious; she doesn't have much of a sense of humor. Evidently she had a very unhappy childhood. She slept with a light on in her room till she was thirty!

Martin helped her put our bags in the back of the car. I sat in the front with Eileen, and Martin sat in the back.

"You poor kids must be zonked," Eileen said. "You can rest the minute we get home."

"Actually, I don't feel that tired," I said, which was true. It was earlier here than in New York, but even so I didn't feel any jet lag yet.

"I'm sorry Harold couldn't make it," Eileen said. "But fortunately I was able to rearrange my patients." Eileen is a psychiatric social worker. She goes to an office part of the time, but sometimes she sees patients at home. Daddy works in an office in San Francisco; he's a lawyer. He's not the kind of lawyer you usually read about who gets up in court and tries to convince people that someone is guilty or innocent. He works with businesses and their legal problems.

When we got back to the house, I began getting excited. Everything looked the same—the living room looking out over the bay, the garden out in back with Eileen's flowers. It's a very pretty modern house. Everything is as sparkling and clean as a picture.

"Ali," said Eileen, "I have a surprise for you—for Martin, too. Where is he?"

"Here I am," said Martin, reappearing. "What happened in there? Everything looks different."

"Well, that's the surprise," Eileen said. "Come on in. I'll show you." She led me toward the back of the house, where the den and guest room used to be. Everything had been redone! For me there was a room with all white furniture, including a four-poster bed. Everything was pink and orange. Even things like the wastebasket matched, and there were curtains with ties in those colors too. It looked exactly like a picture in a magazine.

Eileen was looking at me expectantly, so I said, "Gee, it's really great!" Actually, I was thinking it was too bad I wasn't twelve or even ten because then I might have loved a room like this. But now—well, I have more my own taste and this wasn't exactly it. Now I hate it when things match. I don't know why. It just bothers me. It reminds me of a book I hated when I was little where this grandfather rabbit went around painting shadows on the snow and drops of dew on the flowers. I always thought there was something kind of sick about that idea.

I lugged my bag into the room and started to unpack. Eileen stayed there with me. She showed me where to find the towels and sheets and all of that. Then she sat on the bed and watched me while I put my things away. I wondered if I had made a big enough fuss about the room. Eileen seemed so excited about it. "I always wanted a four-poster bed when I was little," she said. "They're so romantic looking."

"Yeah, it's really nice," I said. "It's beautiful."

"You're looking a little tired, Ali," she said. "Are you sure you don't want to rest?"

"Uh uh," I said.

"This must have been a hard year for you," she went on, "struggling to set up in a new place. That first apartment you had sounded awful!"

The first apartment Mom got us was in a building that had just six floors. In the two months we were there, it seemed like people kept getting robbed or mugged every *second* practically. Nothing bad happened to me, but Mom finally moved us across the street to a brownstone that seemed much safer because there was a special double lock on the outside door. "I sort of got used to it," I said. "The school there is pretty good."

"Wasn't Martin terribly unhappy with it though?" she asked.

"You mean because of the sports thing?"

"Well, I understand the facilities are pretty meager compared to the schools here."

"Yeah, well, I guess." I'm not very good at sports, so it doesn't bother me that much.

"I wish Martin would let Harold send him to Deerfield," Eileen said. "So many boys adore boarding school at that age."

"I guess he didn't know what it would be like," I said, "and now he only has one more year so it doesn't seem worth switching."

"True. But you found it all right? No real problems adjusting?"

Sometimes Eileen talks to me like I'm her patient and she's my doctor. "I got to kind of like it the second term," I said. "It's hard moving in right in the middle of the first term when nobody knows you. I was the only new girl."

I wonder if Daddy and Eileen will ever have children. Eileen is thirty-four, and you'd think if she wanted them, she would do it pretty soon. Mom says that doesn't matter any more. It used to be that women over forty or even thirty-five might have mongoloid babies, but now there's a test they have to find out if the baby has any special problems. I've thought a lot about how I'd feel if Daddy had a child from his second marriage. I think four or five years ago I would have minded a lot, but now I think I could handle it pretty well.

Daddy came home at six thirty. He looked pretty much the same. He has whitish-blond hair—his mother came from Norway—which is getting a little thin on top, but he's nice looking. Not *handsome* in a movie star way, but nice. He hugged me. "Hey, Ali! Look at you! You're gorgeous!"

I turned red. "I grew a little," I said, embarrassed.

"In all the right places, I'd say."

Daddy is somewhat sexist, according to Mom. It's true in a way, I guess. For instance, he looks at pretty girls on the street and says to Martin, "Hey, did you see that one?" and stuff like that.

"Oh goodness, I completely forgot," Eileen said. "Martin, there were two calls for you this week from Tess. She said you—"

"Yeah, I called her," he said.

"And for you, Ali, that friend of yours, the one who's a dancer . . ."

"Gretchen?"

"Yes. She said you should call her as soon as you got in."

I would have called her right then, but Eileen said dinner was ready so we went in to eat.

Daddy and Eileen are really into health food. They don't go to extremes, but they never have butter, just margarine, and Daddy doesn't eat salty things because they're bad for his system. Eileen has an ulcer, so she has to take special pills and drink milk a lot of the time. I think she was a little shocked when I told her Mom lets us eat anything we want and says that we're both disgustingly healthy.

"So, how is the city of grime and crime?" Daddy said. "Still dragging along?"

It's funny. A year ago I would have thought pretty much the same thing. But after living in New York for even one year, I feel indignant when people say how awful it is. Now I just said, "I like it, sort of."

"Think you can survive another year, Marty?" Daddy asked.

"Sure," Martin said. "Anyway, I can't see transferring for just one year."

"That was our big mistake," Daddy said. "I should have just insisted that you go to Deerfield. I knew what New York would be like. I *knew* you'd be miserable."

"I'm not miserable," Martin said.

"It's really nice where we live now," I said, not wanting them to think our lives were so terrible. "Peggy has this apartment next door, and sometimes Mom stays over there so we can have the whole apartment to ourselves. We can even use Peggy's garden—she has one in back."

"Slow down," Daddy said. "First of all, who's Peggy?"

"Mom's friend," I said. "See, we live in this brownstone, and the floor used to be one huge apartment, but they broke it up into little ones. Peggy has one in back and we have one in front."

"Okay, I get that, but what's this about leaving you alone at night?"

"Daddy, they're right there! Don't you get it? They're right next door. Only there was this time when I wanted to have these friends come for a sleep-over party and Mom wanted to work, so Peggy said why didn't *she* stay with her and *we* could stay up as late as we wanted and play music and all that."

"Marty, where were you during this?" Daddy said.

"I was there, in my room."

"Just a bunch of kids all alone in the apartment? Isn't that dangerous?"

"No," I said. "The place is really safe."

"But you said it had a garden in back," Daddy said. "Can't someone climb in that way?"

"No! Daddy, don't be silly. . . . We wouldn't have moved unless Mom was really sure it would be safe. She checked into all of that especially."

"Yes, but Cynthia can sometimes . . . well, anyway, you've been okay?"

"Fine," I said. "Terrific."

He finished off his water. "I still don't get the part about whats-her-name."

"Peggy?"

"Yeah, who *is* she?"

"She lives in our building, I told you."

"She's an art director for some agency," Martin offered.

"How did it come about that she offered Cynthia her apartment then?"

"Well, she's Mom's friend, and I guess it seemed like a good idea," I said, wondering what was so hard for him to understand about that. "See, Mom had this work to do and I was having—"

"I know about that part," Daddy said. "I just don't like the idea of her leaving you two alone."

"They were right next door, Daddy."

"What is Peggy like?" Eileen asked in this almost overly interested way.

"I don't know," I said. "What do you mean?"

"She has a mole on her left ear," Martin said, deadpan.

"Marty," Daddy said sharply. "Eileen's only trying to be nice. Don't talk in that tone of voice, okay?"

"She's nice," I said. "She's, well, not fat or thin, about medium. She has brownish hair and she plays the flute, just for fun though."

"She makes good brownies," Martin said.

"Marty, what was I saying to you just a minute ago?" Daddy said.

"She *does*, Daddy," I said. "She really does. Regular ones and butterscotch."

"She must be very close to Cynthia," Eileen said.

"Yeah, they're good friends," I said. "It's like you and Daddy. Mom says she needs other grown-ups to talk to, not just kids."

"Of course," Eileen said. She smiled at Daddy. "We're glad Cynthia has a friend."

We had dessert, but it was like something had been spoiled. Eileen kept bringing up new topics in this cheerful, strained kind of way, and Martin was mostly silent and just mumbled things at her. I guess Eileen bugs him, but you'd think he'd at least be polite while we're here. Daddy sits there sort of like the referee, trying to make everyone get along. I guess it's hard for him. I mean, he loves Eileen or he wouldn't have married her, so naturally he wants us to love her too, but she's just—well, not such a lovable person. She's nice in some ways, but not lovable. Mom doesn't say that many bad things about Daddy, but I remember she once said Daddy liked bright women who try hard to please and that *she* used to be that way but stopped. She said it got boring, trying to be nice all the time. I don't know if it gets boring for Eileen or not.

After dinner Martin called Tess again; I decided to take a bath. In our bathroom in New York there's just a shower, and I really got to miss taking baths. Eileen had put out special soap and new washcloths; it was really pretty. When I'm in the bath, I tend to daydream. I just lie back and let my hair get wet, though sometimes when it's long—like now—I pin it up and close my eyes. Sometimes I feel like I'm in another place. When I got out, I lay on the bed, wrapped in a towel, thinking about calling Gretchen and wondering if Martin was off the phone yet. He and Tess can stay on the phone for hours. Maybe they like to talk about everything they do under that blanket.

"Ali?" It was Daddy, looking in the door.

I sat up and rearranged the towel around me. "Hi," I said.

"Do you want to be alone?"

"No, not especially."

"Can I come in for a minute?"

"Okay." I felt a little funny wrapped up in just a towel.

"Ali, please try as hard as you can to get along with Eileen this summer. It's a terrible strain for her, on top of her job, to have to deal with the two of you, and—"

"I *am* nice to her," I said. "What was un-nice about anything I did so far?"

"Well, the room, for instance," he said, pointing around him. "She had the feeling you didn't like it, and she spent so much time selecting just what she thought you'd like. She felt really heartbroken at your reaction."

"I *told* her I liked it." I tried to remember what I could have said to make Eileen think I didn't like the room.

"Well, she got the impression you didn't. Now, she *is* terribly sensitive about these things, so maybe just some gesture or expression on your face made her feel that . . ."

I sat there, picking at one of my toenails. "Why is she so sensitive?"

"She's just that way. Look, it means a lot to her to feel that you and Martin really accept her. I guess she felt that before you moved to New York, you were heading in that direction. Now she feels maybe you've become estranged."

"I don't *feel* any different," I said. I sighed. "I'm sorry."

"Right now she's inside with a migraine headache, and I know the whole thing started with this anxiety about the rooms. So could you promise me that no matter what you think about what she's saying or doing, you'll just go along with it? Pretend you think it sounds terrific."

"That's hypocritical," I said.

"Okay. So *be* hypocritical. As a favor to me, okay?"

"But she'll be able to tell."

"Ali, please. You sound so much like Cynthia sometimes."

Knowing how Daddy feels about Mom, I couldn't exactly take that as a compliment. "What's wrong with sounding like Mom?"

"It's just . . . well, you get so defensive as soon as I even make a suggestion. It's just a favor I'm asking that will make everything easier for all of us."

2 7

"But she'll know I'm pretending," I said. "That'll make it worse. You can't pretend to like someone if you don't."

"Well, why *don't* you like her? I don't understand."

I thought a minute. Really, it isn't that I don't *like* Eileen so much as that I never feel *comfortable* with her. Maybe it's because I know she cares so much about my opinions. I feel I have this power over her, and in a way that makes me almost look down on her. "She's okay," I said finally.

Daddy sighed. "I guess I should just give up," he said.

"No, why?" I said. "Daddy, listen, I'll be nice to her. I'll be hypocritical. I don't care."

"Don't think of it as being hypocritical. Think of it as a favor to me. And I think if you'd just get that chip off your shoulder about Eileen, you'd find her a really good friend."

I wasn't so sure about that, but I didn't say anything. Just then something a little embarrassing happened. The towel I was holding slipped and fell to the floor. Daddy and I both reached for it at the same time, and I had it wrapped around me about one second later, but I did feel awkward about him seeing me naked.

"Another thing to remember about Eileen," Daddy went on, as though nothing had happened, "is that she was an only child. So she's not used to all the bickering that goes on between you and Martin—which I'm sure is quite normal, but to unaccustomed ears—"

"Daddy, *he* does it. Why are you talking to me? *He's*

the one. He acts superior all the time, like he was my *teacher* or something."

Daddy raised one hand. "Sweetie, look, I know. Martin has a lot of problems, and I think he does take them out on you sometimes, and even on Eileen. But you also jump back and start in on him instead of at least trying to see his point."

"Okay." I looked up at him, wondering if he was finished. He just stood there.

"Did you have a good year, all in all?" he asked finally.

"I wrote you about it," I said. "Didn't you get my letters?"

"Of course I got them, but apart from the fact that your grades improved, I didn't get a very detailed description of what you were doing."

"It was good. I mean, in the beginning it was bad, not knowing anyone, but since Christmas it's been good."

Daddy didn't speak for a minute. Then he said, "Ali, would you mind—could you go in to Eileen and tell her how much you like the room? I think it would mean a lot to her."

"Can I get dressed first?"

He smiled. "Of course. Look, Eileen *is* hypersensitive in some ways, but give her a chance, okay?"

"Sure."

I changed into my nightgown and then went into Daddy and Eileen's bedroom. It was dark except for this one small light in the corner. Eileen was lying on the bed, a washcloth over her eyes.

"Um, Eileen? It's Ali. Is it okay if I come in?"

Eileen pushed the washcloth down so she could see me. "Hi, Ali."

"Is your headache any better?"

"A little."

"I used to get headaches when I was eleven," I said, "though they were really stomachaches, not headaches. I would get them for the whole day and even at night."

"That must have been awful."

I stood there awkwardly for a minute. "I think Martin and I are going to have a great time this summer," I said. "We're really looking forward to it."

"Alison," Eileen said, pulling the cloth back over her eyes. "We all have to try our best. This isn't easy for me either. Forgive me if I'm impatient or prying. I don't mean to be."

"Sure," I said. I cleared my throat. "I like my room a lot."

"It's Martin who disturbs me," Eileen said. "He's so morose and sullen, like he was angry at someone about something."

"Well, that's his personality," I explained.

"No, it's not. He wasn't like that before."

"He seems the same to me," I said. "I mean it. You shouldn't take it personally."

Eileen smiled wanly. "I do that sometimes, but in this case—well, even Harold has noticed it, just in the few hours you've been here."

Maybe Eileen's right. I just can't tell. I guess I see Martin too much in all kinds of moods to be able to tell if one particular one is worse than the rest. "Maybe I'll go to sleep early tonight," I said.

"That's a good idea," Eileen said. "Well, see you in the morning. Sleep tight."

"You too."

I went inside to call Gretchen. Her line had been busy before supper.

Three

I called Mom after breakfast. It's later in New York than in California, and I'd forgotten to call the night before. By the time I'd thought of it, after talking with Gretchen, it was too late—practically the middle of the night in New York. I had to call Mom at her job, which she doesn't like me to do too much. But she'd said I should feel free to call her any time, even if I was just homesick. I don't feel homesick yet.

"Mom? Hi, it's me. I'm sorry I didn't call you last night."

"That's okay, sweetie. I figured you were probably tired. How're things?"

"Okay," I said. "Eileen fixed up a bedroom just for me, and she did one for Martin in the back where the den used to be. Mine's all decorated and everything. It's orange and pink, with a four-poster bed."

"You're kidding!"

"No, really." I laughed. "It's kind of pretty, in a way."

"Eileen must have really outdone herself for you two," Mom said dryly. "Are you being nice to her?"

"Sure."

"*Be* nice to her, okay? I mean it. She's not exactly the most fascinating person on earth, but just try to act interested. Because, well, anything you do will be placed at my doorstep, as it were. *You* know."

"Daddy said that too—how I should be nice to her. The trouble is, she kind of follows me around, making conversation, you know? I wish she'd just act regular."

"Sweetie, she's doing her best. She's just uptight. It's that whole small-town, white-gloves, I-have-to-do-the-right-thing-if-it-kills-me bit."

"Last night she had a migraine headache, and Daddy said he thought it was because I didn't say I liked the room enough. But I did, Mom, *really*. I said I liked it."

"God, is she *still* getting migraines? Well, I guess life with Harold isn't the most . . . but, hon, try and remember she never had kids. So things *I* might just take in my stride, she—"

"But Peggy never had kids and she's not like that."

"True. Look, it's just—it's her personality. I'm sure she suffers from it more than anyone. How's Harold?"

"He's okay. He's getting a tiny bit bald."

"Huh, poor thing."

"Mom, you know what? I wasn't homesick *before* I called you, but now I am. Maybe I shouldn't have called."

"It's the same with me, sweetie, but it's just for the summer. We'll handle it. Have you seen Gretchen yet?"

"No, I'm going to today. I can hardly wait."

"Give Terry my best if you see her. I've been meaning to write her a letter for ages."

Terry is Gretchen's mother. She and Mom used to be friends. They got to know each other when Gretchen and I met in second grade. I don't think they're good friends the way we are, but they used to talk and compare notes and stuff like that.

"Call whenever you want, Ali, okay? Promise? Don't feel funny about it."

"But don't they mind at your job?"

"Not if it's something important."

"I'm afraid I'll call you too much."

Mom laughed. "You can set reasonable limits."

"Okay. Bye, Mom."

"Bye, sweetie. Take care of yourself. Be well, okay?"

I was glad I was going to see Gretchen. Talking to Mom made me a little sad, though I know I'm much too old to miss her the way I would if I was little. I wish I could be more independent. Mom says the trouble is that at the time of the divorce I was at a sort of clingy stage and maybe I never got out of it. When I was nine and I was still feeling that way, like getting sick in the morning and not wanting to leave her, she took me to see a psychiatrist, and he said to just let me get it out of my system. But the trouble is there are times, not all the time but sometimes, when I feel like I *still* don't have it out of my system. Like, right then, I was glad to be in California, but part of me wanted to go home.

After I finished talking to Mom, I called Gretchen and

she said to come right over. She usually walks part way and we meet at the crossroad that leads down the hill. I started thinking of the time I went to meet Gretchen when I was eleven and had just come home from camp. I'd suddenly gotten breasts over the summer and was so embarrassed for her to see them. Gretchen is very small—small-boned, Mom says—and she has breasts, but they're really small like the rest of her. Mom says that's good. If they were big, she says, they would look funny on a small person. But still, I'll never forget Gretchen's face when she looked at me, like I'd suddenly grown horns or something.

That was the summer people started saying how pretty I was. I can't be objective about it, but I think I look more or less the way I always have. Actually, I think I looked my best when I was about four and had really light blond hair and dark brown eyes, which is an unusual combination. Now my hair is darker—more a dirty blond, like everyone else's. But still, up until that summer no one ever said anything special about my looks, and from then on *everyone* did. I don't like that kind of attention so much, though that's a thing only Gretchen would understand. Maybe if people had been complimenting me all along, since I was *born* or something, I would have been used to it. I don't even like it with boys so much. That is, I wouldn't want to look really ugly, but I'd rather look more in-between so people wouldn't make a fuss about my appearance, as though that was the only interesting thing about me.

I saw Gretchen bouncing along the road as I came

down. She walks with this springy little step, maybe because she's a dancer. When she saw me, she ran over and we hugged and stared at each other and started laughing for no reason.

"Ali! You grew taller!"

"You shrunk."

"I did. You're right! You know the last time I went to the doctor I was five-one and the time after that I was just five feet!" Gretchen really wants to grow so she can be a professional dancer. If she never gets bigger than five-one, that might be a problem.

"Listen, I have something really important to tell you," Gretchen said, "and I have to tell you before we get home because Mom might be there."

I frowned. "They're getting divorced again?"

Last year Gretchen's mother took her and Ethan, Gretchen's brother, aside and said she had decided to divorce Roger. Roger isn't their real father. Their real father was killed in a car crash when they were babies, but they think of Roger as their real father since he married their mother a year later. They talked about it and everything, and then, about two months later, Gretchen's mother decided she *didn't* want to get divorced after all. Gretchen says she just wishes her mother would make up her mind, one way or the other. But she didn't mention anything about it in her letters, so I figured things were okay. Last year, even when her mother was talking about getting divorced, Gretchen was pretty cool about it. She said she'd miss Roger if he moved out though, because she likes him better than her mother.

She shook her head. "She's going to have a baby!"

"Oh, come on! How *can* she?"

"Oh, it's *so* dumb, Ali. It's just to solidify their marriage. I know that, and it won't *work*. She's forgotten what babies are *like*. It's so much work. I do baby-sitting all the time now, and I know. It's just crazy. Ethan thinks so too."

"Why don't you tell her?"

"We did. Both of us talked to her and went over the whole thing about how crazy it was, and all she'd say was that it was good we were getting our resentment out in the open where it could be dealt with. It drives me *crazy!* Anything either of us says she claims is just *our* problem. You know what *really* scares me?"

"Uh uh."

"The baby-sitting. She'll figure she's got a free live-in baby-sitter for the rest of high school!"

"Wouldn't she have to pay you?"

"Oh, you know how it is. Half the time it would be, 'Well, as long as you're going to be home, Gretchen, you might as well keep an eye on little mud face' or whatever they're going to call him. . . . Ali, do I sound unfair? Am I being really selfish thinking of it just from my point of view?"

"No, not at all. I'd feel awful too."

"*Would* you? You're not just saying that?"

I shook my head. "She could get an abortion," I said.

"I know! But it's not that, Ali. She did it on *purpose*."

"You're lucky Ethan feels the same way you do."

Gretchen's face lit up. "Oh, he's been terrific through all of this. He's *so* great, Ali! I mean it. He really gives me the feeling I have an ally, someone to talk to who'll understand."

"I wish *I* felt that with Martin," I said.

"Is he still the same?"

"Pretty much. . . . Wasn't that *weird* about that letter?" I'd written Gretchen about finding Tess's letter.

"Yes! Gee, I never thought Tess was that kind of person."

"What do you mean, 'that kind'?"

"Well, you know, doing all those *things*. I guess I think of girls more like Nancy Simon as, you know . . ."

Nancy Simon was this gross girl who transferred to our class in seventh grade. She had the kind of breasts people call "boobs"—really gigantic ones—and she used to make out with her boyfriend, who was in a class two years ahead of ours, in front of *everybody*. I mean, he'd actually put his hand under her sweater while they were having *lunch!* Still, I felt a little uncomfortable the way Gretchen said that. I think because she's never really liked a boy, she doesn't realize that when you do, all of a sudden you want to do lots of things that never sounded that appealing in the abstract.

By this time we were at Gretchen's house. We went into the kitchen, and Gretchen poured me some Pepsi Light. Then she got the dishwasher going because she'd forgotten to do it before. Her room was the same, kind of messy.

"Do you have any new books?" I asked.

Gretchen and I always tell each other about sexy books we've read and trade them. "Let's see," she said, reaching under her desk. "Yeah, I have a couple. . . . This one is *pretty* good. She gets raped at the beginning. But after that, nothing much happens."

"I wonder if anything is ever going to happen to *us*," I said.

"Well, *you* should talk. You've done more than I have. I haven't done *anything!* Ali, did you really not meet anyone all year like you said in your letters? I couldn't figure out if that was really true or if you just didn't want to say that much in a letter."

"It was true," I said. "Oh, there were a couple of guys I went out with once or twice, but no one that great."

"I think we're both going to spend the rest of our lives saying, 'Next year it'll be different,' " Gretchen said.

I know what she means. I meet plenty of boys, but none of them ever seems half as nice to me as Gretchen. And I'd think to marry someone or even live with them, you'd have to think of them as your best friend.

"I probably won't meet anyone I like until I'm eighty," Gretchen said.

"You can't tell. You might find someone before I do."

"Are you kidding?"

"Wait and see." But I know Gretchen is more worried about it than I am, because she's practically never been out on a real date. When she's with me she's fine and talks a lot, but I've noticed that when boys are around, she gets very quiet and just stands there with a funny expression on her face. Mom says that's just shyness and she'll grow out of it. I'm just the opposite. If I feel nervous, I talk *too* much—just say anything that comes into my head—and sometimes I think that's even worse. At least Gretchen doesn't make an idiot of herself.

"Ali, do you want to swim?"

"I didn't bring my suit. Darn, I meant to."

"You can use one of Mom's. She's more your size."

We went into Gretchen's mother's bedroom, which is always kind of messy. It has a big bright green cover on the bed with lots of small embroidered gray cats crawling up the sides. I don't like Gretchen's mother's suits very much because they were all one-piece and I like bikinis; but if I wore one of Gretchen's bikinis, I'd be hanging out all over the place. So I picked the plainest suit I could find—just a dark blue tank suit. It looked pretty good.

Four

Ethan was outside, reading under a tree. "Hi, Ali," he said. "Long time no see."

"Hi! I just got back yesterday," I said. For some reason with Ethan I feel the way Gretchen says she feels with most boys. I can't think of what to say, and whatever I do think of sounds stupid. He always listens very carefully when you talk, as though he was expecting you to say something important. Maybe that's what makes me nervous.

Ethan and Gretchen look a lot alike, more so than me and Martin. They're both sort of small and delicate looking with straight, shiny black hair and almond-shaped black eyes that tilt up a little when they smile. If you saw Ethan next to Martin, you'd *never* know they were the same age. They used to be in the same class, but they were never that friendly. Martin said Ethan was sort of a loner and not at all interested in sports, which to him practically rules someone out as a friend. Also, I don't think Ethan was ever in the same crowd as

Martin—the boys who dated girls and went to dances and stuff.

"Don't you want to come in?" Gretchen asked. Another thing that Gretchen and Ethan have in common is they both talk very quietly—you have to really listen to hear them.

"I have to do this first," he said, pointing to the book. To me he explained, "I'm tutoring a kid in math this summer, and I have to stay a couple of jumps ahead of him. He's not so dumb actually."

"Then how come he needs tutoring?" I asked.

"Well, it's his mother mostly. She thinks he needs tutoring because he doesn't get all *A*'s in everything."

"Well, Mom's like that," Gretchen said. "When I got that *C* in algebra, she hit the ceiling."

"Maybe with you. With me it's always, 'Why don't you go out and play tennis or baseball, Ethan?' "

"She should have Martin for a son," I said. "Then she'd really be happy."

"Is he still so big on sports?" Gretchen asked.

"Definitely. Only the school we go to in New York isn't so set up for them."

"Do *you* like it though?" Ethan asked.

"Pretty much. It was hard coming in as a new girl. Everyone already had friends. I felt really desperate, so I made friends with these kids who weren't basically that great."

"You shouldn't have, Ali," Gretchen said earnestly. "If you'd waited, someone really nice would have come along."

"I get nervous waiting," I said. "I'm not like you. I can't be patient."

"What's so great about being with a bunch of people you don't even like?" Ethan said. I could see he and Gretchen were looking at me in the same way, as though they couldn't really understand what I meant.

"Well, sometimes you can sort of *get* to like people if you try hard enough."

"Not me," Gretchen said. "If I try, it gets *worse*. I just have to like someone right off, right at the beginning."

"Does your mother like her new job?" Ethan asked.

I nodded. "Yeah, pretty much. She says there's a lot of pressure though."

"Well," Ethan said, standing up, "I guess I better go. See you, Ali."

After he left, Gretchen and I swam and then lay in the sun near the pool. "Remember how we used to wash our hair every Wednesday and let it dry while we sunbathed by the side of the pool?" Gretchen said.

I nodded, feeling sleepy from the sun.

"I ought to do it now," Gretchen said. "My hair's dirty."

"Let's do it," I said, sitting up. I felt dizzy from getting up so quickly.

"For old times' sake?"

"Yeah. Do you still have all those crazy shampoos that smell of avocados and stuff?"

"A few. A strawberry one, I think."

We went inside and washed each other's hair with the special hose Gretchen's mother has in her bathroom. We got sort of giggly and began splashing each other a little, but it didn't matter because we were still in our suits. Then we went outside and sat by the pool again, brushing our hair.

"I heard it's not really good to brush it a hundred times each night," Gretchen said, "so I don't any more. I just brush it when I feel like it."

"Do you still wash it every other day?"

"When I can remember."

I dipped my toe in the pool. "Ethan's *so* nice. You're lucky, Gretchen."

She made a face, more a sad one than anything else.

"How come you're looking that way?"

She sighed. "Listen, promise not to tell this to anyone, Ali?"

"Sure. What though?"

"Well, Mom has been on this strange rampage to get Ethan and me not to be so close. She keeps saying it's unnatural and all that. I think she's just jealous because we've always had each other and all she has is Roger."

"That's really *crazy!*" I said. "I think it's great you can even talk about things like that with him."

"Maybe it was just from her saying that, but I keep wondering if it's true," Gretchen said softly, winding her hair around her finger. "I mean, it *is* true that I've never had a boyfriend, really, and Ethan's never had a girlfriend. Maybe that *is* strange."

"You're both sort of shy," I said. "That's all it is."

"I hope so. It makes me so sick when she brings up things like that. I feel like she's trying to destroy the one good thing in my life besides, well, dancing and you—and you're not even here anymore." Gretchen looked like she was going to cry.

I really felt mad at Gretchen's mother. "She shouldn't say those things to you! But Gretch, how *would* you feel if Ethan ever liked someone? *Would* you be jealous?"

"If *I* didn't have someone too? Yeah, sure."

There was a pause.

"Well, anyway, he doesn't," I said.

She looked up at me, frowning. "He will someday."

"But so will you."

"I don't *know*, Ali. Everybody *says* that all the time, but I'm beginning to wonder if I'm just sort of weird."

"You're *not!*"

"The thing is, I want to really *like* someone as a person first. I couldn't just go out with someone I didn't feel really close to, the way you did with Teddy."

I blushed. It's true, I guess. If Teddy hadn't been so good looking and such a good kisser, maybe I wouldn't have gone out with him so much.

Toward suppertime Gretchen's mother came home. Since Gretchen had said she was pregnant, I thought she'd look that way, but she didn't. She's small, like Gretchen and Ethan, with lots of frizzy black hair that fluffs out around her head, and big, blue-tinted, aviator-style glasses. She wears a lot of eye makeup and kind of kooky clothes. Like today she was wearing a white jumpsuit with little red frogs all over it and white high-heeled sandals. I guess one reason she looks like that is because she's an actress. Mostly she acts in musical comedies. She's always going out for auditions, Gretchen says. That's where you try out; and if they like you the best, you get the part.

"So you finally made it, Ali," she said, giving me a hug. "Welcome back! We've missed you."

"I've been missing all of you too," I said.

"Gretch, where's Ethan?"

"He's tutoring."

"Oh right. Honey, listen, would you mind dropping down to the Supermart and getting me a couple of things? It's not much. Just some eggs and yogurt."

"I'll go with you," I said.

We changed in Gretchen's room. She was really tan. You could see the places where her bathing suit ended, but I was as pale as a fish.

"It's funny that your hair down there is so light," Gretchen said, looking at me. "I mean, compared to your other hair."

"My hair used to be really blond," I said. "Didn't I show you those pictures of me when I was four or something?"

"I can't get used to having hair there," Gretchen said. "When my mother used to go around naked, I always thought that part of her looked funny."

Mom doesn't usually go around without her clothes on. "I guess I don't mind it so much," I said.

"See what I mean about being strange though, Ali? Like, you think it's great and I can't get used to it."

"Quit picking on yourself," I said. "I mean it, Gretch. That's all you're doing."

"I guess. That's what Ethan says too," Gretchen said pensively. "He says it's dumb because enough bad things happen in life anyway without looking for them."

"He's right. He's really smart—I mean it. Maybe he should be a psychiatrist when he grows up."

"I bet he'd be good," Gretchen said. "Once Mom had me go to this counselor at school, you know? About the time they were going to get divorced and all. And he wasn't half as smart as Ethan, not *half*."

"I believe you."

Gretchen had her shorts and T-shirt on again. Her hair was so short that it was dry already, even though we'd been swimming just a little while earlier.

"Ali?" Gretchen said suddenly in a more worried voice again.

"Yeah?"

"Oh, Ali, maybe I shouldn't tell you this. I promised Ethan I wouldn't tell anybody."

"What is it?"

"It's just . . . remember that man we saw Mom with in the restaurant last year—when she said it was just someone she worked with?"

"Yeah."

"Well, it turns out she had an affair with him or something. That's what she and Roger were yelling about all the time. Once we heard this whole screaming bout they had, and Roger kept bringing that man up, and she started to cry and yell. It was awful!"

"So, how come she and Roger got back together again?"

"I guess she stopped seeing him. But it's so *weird*—it seems so weird to me, doesn't it to you?" She sighed. "Oh Ali, why'd you have to move away? I feel like this is the first time all year I've talked to anyone about all this stuff, except for Ethan. I really missed you!"

"Me too. I don't talk to anyone in New York the way I talk to you. I mean, they're friends, but not in that special way."

"I wish we were in college already and could be together all the time," Gretchen said. "Won't that be great?"

"Well, we can be . . . in a couple of years."

"That's so far away, though. Oh, I know I'm being silly, but I just—" Gretchen started to cry.

I hugged her. "Gretchen, come on, *don't*. I'm here *now*. That's what counts, isn't it? And we have all summer."

Gretchen sniffed. She looked up at me with her big black eyes. Her eyelashes were still wet. "Don't tell anyone any of the stuff I told you, okay?"

"Of course not! What do you think?"

"There are *good* things about Mom too. Don't think I just think—"

"I know. Listen, I kind of like your mother. When I was little, I used to wish my Mom was like her."

"You did?"

"Yeah. Your mother always seemed so peppy and pretty, sort of jazzy."

"Really? I always wished mine would be more like yours—calm and organized and *sane*."

4 8

We both laughed.

It's funny how if you're really close to someone, even if you haven't seen them in a year, you can catch up so fast and it seems like you were only away about a day. That's how I felt when I came home from Gretchen's, like we had just seen each other at school around a week ago.

Five

"How come you didn't tell me when you were coming, Ali?"

"I wasn't sure till the last minute, Teddy. That's all."

"Well, we're going to see each other, aren't we? I've got a job in the afternoons, but on weekends I thought we could."

"Sure." I began doodling on a pad near the phone.

"You don't sound that enthusiastic. Did you meet some other guy in New York?"

"Uh uh."

"So, how about Saturday? Do you want to see a movie?"

"Okay. Or we could just walk around a little and talk."

"I'll come by at eight. How's that?"

There's one thing about Teddy I never told anyone, not even Gretchen, because I was afraid she'd make fun of him. It's really weird. He has this scrapbook that he calls "our scrapbook," and in it he puts all these things about what our life together will be like in the future. Like, if he sees a house that he thinks we might live in, he puts that in. Or a dog we might have. Or some place in the United States where he thinks it would be good to live. He does it in this very calm, scientific way. I told him a million times that I don't know if I am going to marry him, but he still kept on the same way about it. I bet he still has that scrapbook, even though I've been away all year. I guess I should be flattered, but it seems sort of crazy to me, wanting to plan out your whole life when you're just fifteen years old.

On Saturday, Tess came for dinner. Every time I look at Tess, I think of that letter and get embarrassed. She really does seem like a nice person.

"How's the tennis going, Tess?" Daddy asked. He plays tennis too, but he's not really good like Tess and Martin.

"She won the intrastate championship," Martin said proudly.

"I've been working at it all year," Tess said.

"You should see her serve," Martin said. "It's a real cannonball."

Tess gave him a shy glance. "Are *you* playing, Ali?" she asked.

"No, not much." In New York you can get a permit and play in the park, but since we were going to be here all summer I figured it didn't pay.

"I played in the park till Thanksgiving," Martin said. "I played right on Thanksgiving day, remember, Ali?"

"It was freezing! You were crazy." I remember how I stayed behind to help Peggy fix the turkey while Martin went out looking like he was going skiing—with his parka on and these gloves and everything.

"You know, all the courts were taken," Martin said. "Every single one."

"So. New York is full of crazy people," Daddy said.

"No more than here," I said quickly.

"I wish *I* could take up tennis," Eileen said, "but I'm so lazy when it comes to sports. I see the ball and I know I should try to run fast, but then I figure: Why bother? You can't be a good player that way."

"No," Martin said. "You have to really care. I think that's why Tess is better than me. She cares more."

"I don't know," Tess said. "You care about other things, like school. My grades are so awful. I mean, not really terrible, but I just know that I could study forever and still not be good at those things."

Daddy stood up and stretched. "Are the three of you going to a movie tonight?"

Martin looked horrified at the idea of having to spend an evening with me.

"No, Teddy's coming," I said.

Daddy smiled. "Teddy, Teddy. How could I forget Teddy?" he said.

"Daddy, don't," I said. I hate it when he teases me.

Martin and Tess went out before Teddy came. I sat in my room listening to records with the sound on not too loud so I'd hear him when he rang the doorbell. Daddy peeked in.

"Ali?"

"Yeah?"

"Don't stay out too late, will you?"

"Daddy, come on! Why does it matter? It's vacation."

"It's the principle of the thing. You need sleep to stay healthy. If I return you to Cynthia looking like a wreck, she'll hit the ceiling."

"She said I could stay up as late as I wanted," I said. Really, that's kind of a lie, but I knew Daddy wouldn't bother checking it.

"Every night?" Daddy said, looking suspicious.

"No, for special occasions. But this *is* one. I haven't seen Teddy since last year."

"Can we agree on midnight?"

"Okay." I just hate the idea of having to be back at a certain time. It isn't even that I want to stay out till then. It's more that I have the feeling Daddy still thinks of me as a baby, and that bothers me.

When Teddy came, I showed him my new room. I closed the door behind us. Teddy kissed me. He always smells good, of shampoo and everything. I know he really cares how he looks, just as much as I do. I think boys do care about those things, even though they say they don't. I feel bad in a way because I can't honestly decide if I'd like Teddy if he wasn't so good looking. I know that's a terrible reason to like someone. He has dark blond hair and really blue eyes, like Paul Newman, and freckles and a great smile. When he kisses me, I get a funny feeling—good but funny.

We did end up going to a movie, but then we decided to walk back to the house because it wasn't even eleven yet.

"Why'd you stop writing to me?" Teddy asked. We

5 3

were holding hands and walking along real slowly. "I couldn't figure it out. It was okay up till Christmas, but then you kind of kept waiting longer and longer to answer my letters."

"You wrote back so fast!" I said. "I didn't have a chance with all the homework and stuff I was getting."

"Did you have a lot?"

"Tons of it. Mom said it was supposed to be this open school, but we got more work than here, we really did—tons of math and book reports and everything."

"I guess my letters weren't so interesting," Teddy said with a slightly doleful expression.

I squeezed his hand. "They *were*, really. I liked getting them."

Teddy put his arm around me and leaned over to kiss me, first on the cheek and then on the lips. When Teddy kisses me, he gets this very serious expression. "You smell good," he said in a husky voice.

"Thanks."

"Boy, imagine if you'd moved away for good, not even coming back for summers!"

"Then I'd never see Daddy," I said.

"Or me."

"Yeah, well . . ." I started feeling uncomfortable about all the times I hadn't even thought of Teddy. "That's funny what you wrote about Sheila and Elvis breaking up."

Sheila and Elvis were these kids in our class who were practically planning to get married and everything.

"She just met someone else, I guess. She wouldn't even give him a reason."

"Someone from school?"

"Uh uh . . . from some party she went to." He kicked a rock in the road. "I hate it when girls do that!" he said angrily.

"Do what?"

"Just suddenly change like that, when they used to like someone, suddenly not like a guy any more, with no warning or *anything*. Boys aren't like that."

"They are *so!*"

"No, they aren't. If a boy says he likes someone, he really means it. Boys don't tease around the way girls do."

"Teddy, that isn't true! Boys drop girls just as fast if they meet someone they like better."

"*I* wouldn't," he said intensely, looking right at me.

"You can't tell."

After a second he said, "I did go out with Emily a couple of times."

"Emily Newman?"

"Yeah."

Emily Newman is this skinny girl who wore her hair in braids up till sixth grade practically. I guess she had a crush on Teddy. Whenever she saw us together, she'd kind of suck on her lower lip and scowl.

"You always said you couldn't stand her," I reminded him.

He looked a little embarrassed. "No, *I* never minded

her. *You* were the one who used to say all that stuff about her, not me."

"Okay, I don't care. So you went out with her, so what. Was it fun?"

"Ali, don't get mad. It was just a couple of times, that's all."

"I'm *not* mad. I went out too, with lots of different people."

"Did you really like them or was it just to—"

"Just to what?"

"Just to tell me about when you got back?"

"Teddy, what do you think I *am?* Of course, it wasn't that! I just wanted to get to know people at the new school. It wasn't just boys. I needed girls for friends since Gretchen wasn't around."

"Gretchen!" he said.

"What about her?"

"She's so weird. I can't figure out why you're still friendly with her."

"I *love* her! She's my best friend. You don't even know her or you wouldn't say things like that."

We were back at my house.

"Can I, um, come in?" Teddy asked uncertainly.

I shrugged my shoulders.

"Ali, come on. Let's not fight. Why should I have to like Gretchen just because you do? You don't like all *my* friends."

"Well, but you're not friends with them the way I am with Gretchen. You don't love them. They're more just guys to hang around with."

"I don't know how you can say you *love* Gretchen. That sounds crazy!"

"I do. Who says you can only love people in your own family? You can love friends."

"Maybe," he sighed.

"I thought tonight was going to be so great, our first night together."

I stood there without saying anything. I felt bad too.

He looked at me with this sort of pleading expression. "Why don't I just come in for a little while, okay?"

"Okay."

We went into my room, and Teddy sat down next to me on the floor. I just didn't feel in the mood for making out that much, although I knew he expected it. He put his arms around me. "I guess I shouldn't have told you about Emily," he said.

"I don't care about her, Teddy. I told you that!"

"I bet you do."

"Listen, it's *your* bad taste. It has nothing to do with *me*."

"She really likes you, Ali. I know you won't believe that."

"She never *acted* like she did."

"She said that was just because you acted stuck up with her."

"She's just dumb. Maybe if I was really desperate, I'd have her for a friend, but not otherwise."

"Remember that time you ran for class president and she beat you? That's how come you're still mad at her, I bet."

"It is not! I just don't like her. Why should I like everyone on the whole face of the earth?"

Teddy began stroking my arm softly up and down; his face was right next to mine. "Ali, seriously, I'm sorry I took her out."

"Don't be sorry."

"I am, I mean it." He looked down at me with his blue, blue eyes. "Do you believe me?"

"I guess," I said, getting a kind of melting feeling despite myself. "But that isn't what I was mad about."

"What is, then?"

"I don't like what you said about Gretchen."

"Okay, I take it back."

"You're just saying that. You don't really mean it."

"Well, I can't pretend to like her if I don't, can I? I just wish I hadn't said anything to you about her."

"If people are shy, they just act a certain way; they can't help it. That doesn't make them weird."

"Yeah, I know."

Suddenly I was tired of talking to Teddy. It seemed like we couldn't talk about *anything* without arguing.

"Let's stop talking," he said all of a sudden.

"Okay." I looked up at him.

"Oh, Ali!" Teddy said, putting his arms around me.

The rest of the evening wasn't so bad. We sat around kissing and making out and stuff. That part is always good. Maybe if we could just never talk, that would be the best. Teddy is pretty good about not pressuring me to go any further than I want to. We've always kept our clothes on. Once or twice we almost broke down and took them off, but I always backed off. I figure if I can't decide about it, I'm not ready. Teddy says he knows that someday I'll want to do it and it doesn't matter if we wait. He's willing to be patient, he says.

Six

One morning, after we'd been in Berkeley about three weeks, I went into the kitchen for breakfast. Martin was already up.

"Hi," I said. "You're up early." It was only seven. Usually Martin likes to sleep late on vacations and weekends.

He poured himself some milk. "Well, actually, I'm just going to sleep."

"What?"

He smiled sheepishly. "Well, it's vacation and all that."

"You've been up all *night?*"

"Yeah."

"Where?"

"At Tess's."

"Don't her parents mind?"

He hesitated. "Promise not to mention this to anyone?"

"Sure."

"Well, they're away for two weeks."

"Aha! What about her brother?"

"He's at camp."

"So, you just, like, stay there?"

"Right. Only I try and get back before they get up," he said, nodding toward Daddy and Eileen's room.

"So, it's sort of like being married," I said, musing.

Martin made a face. "Not exactly."

"Well, sort of. I mean, if you see the person in the morning before they've brushed their teeth and all that."

"Oh, yeah . . . from that point of view."

"Do you think you *will* marry her?"

Martin shrugged. "I don't know."

"You love her, don't you?"

"Sure, but I'm not going to go rushing into marriage when I'm not even twenty. I mean, I figure I'll get married at thirty or something."

"That's a long time," I said. "Would Tess wait that long?"

"She doesn't know either. I guess I just wish—"

"What?"

"That we could be together more."

"You mean, like if you lived out here?"

"Yeah."

I stared at him. "You'll be in college in a year."

"Sure. Only I don't know if we'll go to the same place. Tess wants to go to the University of Colorado."

"How come?"

"Her parents went there." He yawned. "Well, anyway . . ."

Martin went in to go to sleep, and I went to get

dressed. I felt good about his talking to me that way since he doesn't do it very often. Just as I finished dressing, Eileen looked in and asked if I wanted to go shopping with her. I'd told her I needed a new bathing suit.

"I'm supposed to go to Gretchen's around lunchtime though," I said.

"That's okay," she said. "I don't have any patients this morning."

Eileen and I have been getting along pretty well. I've been trying to do what Daddy said, give her a chance, and it seems to be working.

"What style suit were you thinking of getting?" Eileen asked as we entered the store.

"A bikini, I guess," I said.

Eileen looked worried. "You don't think a tank suit would be more practical?"

"Why?"

"Well, I just thought . . . don't bikinis tend to slip off while you're swimming?"

"No, and you can get them in two different sizes," I explained, "if you're smaller on top than on bottom or vice versa."

"Oh. Well, that's good."

Eileen doesn't like sexy clothes that much. One night last week I went out to eat with her and Daddy. I put on all that Bloomingdale's makeup I'd brought along—blusher and eye shadow—and I wore a really cute scoop-necked dress I got this spring. Eileen kept saying, "Don't you think it would look better with a bra?" The thing is, it's not the kind of dress you can wear with a bra because it's cut low on the sides. I think she just said that because the headwaiter in the restaurant came over when we were done eating and went into this long speech about how important it was to him to get fresh fruit and vegetables and things for the restaurant. All the while he was talking, he kept looking down the front of my dress! Eileen got very huffy about it and said she would never go back there, but Daddy just smiled and said she should take these things more lightly. Then when we got home, he came into my room and asked in this sort of embarrassed voice if I didn't think I might "take a little tuck" in the front of the dress. "It's a very pretty dress though," he said.

The point is, I know I have a good figure. Is it my fault if dumb men like to stare at my breasts? That's *their* problem! I hate wearing bras in the summer anyway, because they get all sweaty and stick to you. Eileen says it's vulgar to have your nipples showing through a T-shirt, but I just don't see why. What's so vulgar about nipples? Babies drink from them, don't they?

Eileen came into the dressing room with me. I tried on the three suits I liked best. "I think I like the green one," she said.

I knew she'd like that one. It was hardly even a bikini. It was more shorts and a halter top. I knew that this would be a perfect time for me to be nice to Eileen and

63

get the suit she liked best, but I just couldn't—I really didn't like it. "I think I like this one best," I said pointing to the black one.

"Isn't black a little, sophisticated?"

"What do you mean?"

"Well, I just thought . . . this one with the little strawberries on it is more what I'd imagine someone your age wearing."

I wrinkled my nose. "I don't like that one. It looks kind of. . . . Anyway, black looks good with a tan."

Eileen was silent a moment. "How much *is* the black one?"

It was twenty-three dollars, but so were the others. It does seem a lot to pay for such a little bit of material. Eileen said it would be a treat from her.

Then we went to the underwear department. She got some bra-slips and I got a lightweight one-size-fits-all bra. "That shouldn't encumber your movements that much," she said wryly.

"It's not that," I started to say, but then I decided not to argue about it. Just because I have it doesn't mean I have to wear it.

"It's so much fun having you here this summer, Ali," Eileen said in the car as we drove back after lunch. "I just wish you could come on vacations as well."

"Me too," I said.

"I think it's especially hard for Harold," she said, glancing over at me. "He feels like he's sort of gotten out of touch with you these past few years."

"Yeah, well . . ." I didn't know exactly what to say.

"It's his work, partly," Eileen said. "It's so demanding. And then, when you were small, he was trying to get established."

"I know." Mom says the same thing about Daddy, how she thinks he didn't do enough with us when we were small. "Is he established now?"

"Yes, well, he's certainly . . . but I guess one thing leads to another. There doesn't seem to be any *end* to it."

I thought of how Ethan once said he didn't see how people could stand a nine-to-five job because they'd never be out of doors or anything. "Is he sorry he's a lawyer?" I asked.

"No, not *sorry*. But he feels he missed out on that time when both of you were growing up."

"With Martin too?"

"Yes, with both of you."

It was funny to be hearing all this from Eileen. I didn't see why Daddy didn't say it to us, if he felt it.

"It must be really hard on Cynthia," Eileen said, "coping with the two of you alone in New York."

"Yeah, I guess. She doesn't mind it though. Without us she might've been lonely."

Eileen smiled. "True."

"Do you think you'll ever have a baby?" I asked, hoping that wasn't too personal a question.

"I've thought of it," Eileen said slowly, "but I'm just not sure—all that responsibility. I'm such a perfectionist about everything."

"Babies aren't that hard," I said encouragingly.

Eileen smiled. "How do you know?"

"From baby-sitting." I turned to face her. "You learn to change their diapers and give them bottles. I can handle a baby perfectly well, and I didn't know *anything* about it in the beginning." I told her about this lady I baby-sat for in New York who had a baby only six weeks old. He was still sleeping in this box they brought him home from the hospital in. "They're cute when they're little," I said.

"You make it sound so easy, Ali. When it's your own, you worry much more. You have to, it's inevitable."

"I don't see why. *I* wouldn't."

"You're too young to really understand what being a parent is like."

"No I'm not." I meant that too. "I can imagine it, I can, really." Sometimes when I'd baby-sit for the Carlsons, I'd pretend their baby was mine. I want to have at least two children when I grow up.

Eileen dropped me at Gretchen's house since we got back a little later than I expected. "Let's do this again," she said as I got out. "We could get you a few things for the fall. Now's a good time."

"Sure," I said, taking the bag with my bikini in it. "Thanks for the suit."

Nobody answered when I rang the bell, so I went out back. Ethan was sitting under that same tree reading.

"Where's Gretchen?" I asked.

"She had to go out—to get sneakers, I think."

"She told me to come after lunch." I stood there hesitantly, wondering what to do.

"You can stay, Ali," Ethan said. "Go swim if you like."

"Are you sure? I might disturb you."

"Go on. Don't be silly."

I went to Gretchen's room and changed into my new suit. I cut the price tag off with her nail scissors. Then I looked at myself in the full-length mirror on the closet door. I looked good. Maybe this is a vain thing to tell about, but once in gym the teacher was weighing us and seeing how tall we were and when she came to me she said, "You have a perfectly proportioned body. Do you exercise a lot?" I felt awful because I never exercise at *all!* But I said I played tennis a little. "Well, whatever you're doing, it's the right thing," she said. "Keep up the good work." I do think of that sometimes when I look at myself without clothes on. And I have to admit that I did look sort of sexy in that suit. It has these little ties at the sides that loop down a little, and on top there's a round brass ring between the breasts.

When I went outside, Ethan looked up again. I was hoping he'd say something about my suit, that it looked nice or something, but he just smiled and went on reading. I guess he's not the type to notice that sort of thing so much. Teddy would. Still, you'd think just to be polite, he'd say *something.* Anyway, *I* think it's a nice suit even if he doesn't. I can almost understand the way Teddy feels about Gretchen in relation to how I feel about Ethan. I know he's not stuck up, maybe just shy, but he always makes me feel like I'm doing something wrong. I swam around a little and then climbed out to dry off on the edge of the pool. Ethan was looking up again so I said, "How's your tutoring going?"

"I like it," Ethan said. "He's really beginning to catch on to it now. In the beginning it seemed impossible."

"It must be like being a teacher," I said. "I'd hate that."

"Why?"

"Oh, you know, I just wouldn't ever want to be one."

"I would," Ethan said. "I sometimes think I'll be a teacher after college."

"What kind?"

"Maybe of little kids, five or six. They're so great at that age."

I never thought of a man teaching first grade. All my teachers were women except for Mr. Prior, the science teacher. I always thought men would be bored teaching little kids.

"I bet you'd be good at it," I said.

"If you can get them to respond, it's such a terrific feeling," Ethan said. His eyes lit up. "Of course, it doesn't always work. What do you think *you'll* do after college?"

"I don't know." I went over and sat down next to him.

"Don't you ever think about it?"

"I guess I'd like to be a news announcer on TV."

"Why that?"

The reason I thought of that is sort of dumb. First, a few people have told me I look like Jane Pauley on the "Today" show. I don't think I look exactly like her, but I know what they mean. And then once our drama teacher said I had a good voice. He didn't think I was such a good actress, but he thought my voice had a lot of "timbre." But all I said to Ethan was, "I'd earn lots of money that way."

"Does that matter a lot to you?"

I smiled. "Well, it might be nice. I mean, I could have a terrific apartment and a car and everything."

"True."

"Or maybe I'll just get married. But I think I want to have a job too. I want to do everything."

Ethan laughed. "I bet you will."

I blushed.

"I hope Gretchen will be okay," he said a moment later, looking worried.

"What do you mean?"

"Oh, about all of that—dating, marriage. She's so shy. I worry about her a lot."

I think it's really great that Ethan cares enough about Gretchen to worry about her. "Sometimes, in books, those people get married first," I said, trying to be hopeful. I kept thinking of all the things Teddy said about Gretchen, about how she was so weird, and it made me feel bad even thinking about it.

"I'm sorry to hear about your mother and the baby," I said, just to change the topic.

Ethan smiled ruefully. "There *are* saner families on the face of the earth. Someplace, there's got to be."

"Are you scared she'll make you baby-sit a lot?"

He shook his head. "I just think she and Roger should

have gotten divorced. It's awful hearing them argue all the time. Every time they begin yelling, Gretchen gets sick."

"I didn't know that," I said, frowning.

"It's this back and forth thing they keep pulling. Just as soon as they've seen the light, one of them decides they really need each other, quote unquote, and they come back together again. Then, after five seconds they're screaming again."

I ran my fingers through the grass. "It's funny," I said. "I don't even remember when Mom and Daddy were together."

"Don't you?" Ethan said. He brushed the hair out of his eyes. "Maybe you're lucky."

"No, I wish I *did* remember, even the bad parts. Because it's like it never happened if you can't remember. Mom will start talking about stuff that happened when she and Daddy were together, and I don't remember a single thing! You know the way they say something will come back to you if you try hard enough? Well it's not true because I've tried. And I still draw a complete blank." I stopped abruptly. Ethan was gazing at me pensively. I couldn't tell what he was thinking.

"What are you thinking about?" he said.

I didn't know if I should tell him. "I always thought you would be hard to talk to, but you aren't." After I said it, I felt embarrassed, afraid he might get mad.

"I thought the same thing about you," he said.

"*Me?*" I was so surprised. "People say I never *stop* talking."

"You don't usually talk about personal things."

"With Gretchen I do."

He looked at me, hesitated, and then said, "Are you still seeing that guy?"

"Teddy?"

"Yeah. From what Gretchen said it sounded like you really liked him."

"Well, sort of," I said.

He frowned. "What do you mean, 'sort of'?"

"No, I *like* him. I just don't know if I *love* him or anything like that. Probably I should, but I don't."

"Why should you?"

"Well, he's nice to me and I've known him so long, since fourth grade."

"You can outgrow people," Ethan said.

"I know," I said, feeling I was betraying Teddy by agreeing. "Did *you* ever do that?" I asked. "Outgrow somebody?"

"Not in the way you're thinking of," he said. After a second he added, "I don't go out on dates."

"How come?"

"I don't know." He looked embarrassed. "I just never did."

"Aren't you even curious to know what it's like?"

"In a way."

We just sat there, staring at each other. Ethan is about my height, so we were looking right into each other's eyes. I started getting a funny feeling. Just then Gretchen drove up with her mother.

"Hi, Ali," she said, getting out of the car.

"Hey, what a darling suit!" her mother said. "Is it new?"

I nodded. "I just got it with Eileen."

"*Very* sexy. Don't you think, Ethan?"

Ethan kind of mumbled something. I saw Gretchen make a face like: Don't mind her. I felt funny. I got worried Gretchen wouldn't like the fact that I'd been there, talking with Ethan. Maybe she'd be jealous or something. I wondered if I'd been flirting with him. Sometimes it's hard to tell. You start off having a regular conversation, but you end up flirting. At least I do. Usually it wouldn't matter, but with Ethan I felt more awkward from worrying about what Gretchen would think.

"When did you get here?" she asked.

"I came after lunch," I said. "Eileen dropped me off after we went shopping."

She raised her eyebrows. "That suit is really something."

I decided to take that as a compliment. "Did you get sneakers?"

"Yeah, and a pile of other stuff. I'll go inside and change."

Ethan and I sat there in silence. It was like the mood had been broken. "I forget what we were talking about," I said, just to say something.

"Me too," he said. "It doesn't matter."

All of a sudden a horrible thought came to me. What if I started liking Ethan, *really* liking him and he liked me? Gretchen would die! I felt so guilty just *thinking* about it. I wished I hadn't even started talking to him.

Gretchen came out with the new issue of *Playgirl*.

"Oh no," Ethan said, smiling.

"What do you mean 'Oh no'!" Gretchen said indignantly. "Some of them are nice."

"It's educational," I said, smiling at him.

"Sure." He stood up. "Okay, kids, so long."

The way he said "kids" made it seem like before—as though we hadn't had that personal talk at all. I felt better.

Gretchen and I sat near the pool and looked at *Playgirl*.

"I wonder why they have so many men with moustaches," I said.

"I guess women like them."

"I don't, at *all*. Do you?"

"Well, Roger has one and he looks nice with it."

"True, I forgot about that. God, look at *him*! He's *weird!*"

"I know! He doesn't have any hair on his chest or anything."

"I don't like it when they're all *covered* with hair, but still . . ."

We looked at some more pictures of that man. "Does it mean he has an erection if his penis is pointing up like that?" I asked.

"I don't know. I guess so."

"How do you think they get him to have one? Show him dirty pictures or something?"

Gretchen smiled. "Maybe the photographer was a naked lady."

"Hey, I never thought of that. God, that one's really gross!"

"I *know!* He looks like he's wearing eye makeup or something." She closed the magazine. "Some months they have terrible ones."

"You know, Martin got this issue of *Playboy* that had college girls in it, real college girls, people getting their law degrees at Oxford and stuff."

"Really?" Gretchen made a face. "I bet it wasn't true."

"No, it *was.* That was the whole point."

"I can't imagine anyone smart doing that, can you?"

"You mean posing?"

"Yeah. Would you, if they asked you?"

I thought a minute. "Well, maybe if I knew I'd never meet anyone who'd seen the picture of me."

"I'd *never* do it," Gretchen said vehemently, "not if they paid me a million dollars!"

I know this is an awful thing even to think, but Gretchen really doesn't have that sexy a figure and I don't think anyone *would* pay her a million dollars. "Well, I guess I wouldn't be that eager to either," I said.

She wrinkled her nose. "Think of having all those gross men gawking at some photo of you in a bubble bath!"

"Maybe they're not gross," I said. "I mean, *we're* looking at these pictures and *we're* not gross."

"That's different," she said.

"How?"

"Well, we're not . . . I mean, we're not *drooling* over them or imagining *doing* anything with them. We're just looking."

"That's true," I said. But I felt awful because actually there is this one man they had a few issues ago that I do think about when I'm masturbating sometimes. He had this very understanding expression. You could tell he'd be a very nice person, but he also was really good looking, sort of like an older, more sensitive version of Teddy. I hope that doesn't mean something terrible about me, that I do that.

Gretchen was looking at me with a serious expression. "What were you talking about with Ethan?" she asked.

"Nothing special," I said.

"You both looked so serious when we drove up, like you were discussing something really important."

I cleared my throat. "Uh uh. I don't even remember what it was."

"I sound like I'm jealous, which is so dumb," she said. "Don't I?"

"Well, just a little bit," I said carefully.

"I've sometimes imagined what would happen if you and Ethan liked each other—the two people I like the most going off without me."

"Don't worry," I said quickly.

"I'm crazy, I guess," Gretchen said, pulling on her shirt. "Ugh, today was a mess."

"What happened?"

"Mom!" she said. "She drives me crazy. She said she'd drive me in and just buy sneakers and some sandals she wanted. Because I knew you were coming over. Well, suddenly she decided she had to get maternity clothes because she gave all her old stuff away when she figured she wouldn't have any more kids. So we get to the store and everyone keeps thinking it's *me* that's pregnant, and salesladies keep coming over and looking worried, like: Who is this poor little creature that got pregnant? Mom doesn't even *show* that much yet. I don't see why she needs maternity clothes."

"Did she get any?"

"Yeah, some really ugly things. They make her look like she's going to have a whole *litter* or something."

I laughed. "I went shopping with Eileen today," I said. "It wasn't so bad."

"Is she still bugging you?"

"Not as much."

"Ali?"

"Yeah?"

"Do you ever wonder what it was like when your parents got along? Like, before they were married and just in love or something?"

"Sometimes."

"I wish we could have it on a movie so it would seem real because I just can't imagine Mom and Roger ever getting along. But they must have. I mean, they didn't get married because Mom was pregnant, so it must have been because of love."

"I guess people just make mistakes," I said.

"I guess. . . . How's Teddy, speaking of love?"

"Come on, Gretch, I don't *love* him and I never did. I *told* you that! We have fun together, that's all."

She just looked at me. I don't think it's so bad just to like having fun with someone. I mean, I'm only fifteen. If I don't have fun now, when will I?

Seven

Daddy and Eileen ate out Tuesday night, which meant Martin and I had to make dinner for ourselves. He bought a big steak and we shared it, along with frozen french fries, which I heated up, and a salad made of some crinkly lettuce that Eileen said we could use. Martin had a bottle of beer and I had a Pepsi Light.

I've been thinking a lot about liking Ethan. I just can't get it out of my head. It's really terrible because whenever I try to think of something else, that's *all* I can think of. I keep trying to argue myself out of it. First of all, he's not especially handsome. Teddy's *much* better looking and has a better body and everything. Ethan is sort of small. He's barely over my height, which is only five-five, and he's too thin. I really like his smile, though, and I like the way he listens when I talk.

What's bad about liking Ethan is I don't have anyone to talk to about it. Usually I'd talk to Gretchen, but I can't now because she would feel so bad. I know she'd take it the way she said—that we were going off and deserting her in some way. I really don't feel I like

Gretchen any *less* because of this, not at all—but she might not understand that.

Once Gretchen and I had an awful argument. We went to some dance together, and I guess I was acting silly with the boys, laughing a lot, I don't even remember. But she said afterward how she hated being with me when I was like that, that she felt ashamed of how silly I was, how I just put on a big act with boys and it wasn't my "real" personality at all. I was really hurt. I think it's a little bit true, only I don't see what's so bad about pretending as long as you *know* it's pretending and can go back to your real self with people you really like. But Gretchen said she'd heard of people who never could go back. They forgot who their true self *was!* At the time, I did kind of think that maybe Gretchen was jealous of me, that maybe she wanted to act silly at times but just couldn't. But I felt hurt anyway.

The funny thing is I sort of like Ethan *because* of my friendship with Gretchen. It's not just that I'd never have met him otherwise, but he's connected in my mind with her because they're sort of alike. I mean, I don't know Ethan half as well as I know Gretchen, but I feel I know more about him indirectly because Gretchen is always talking about him.

Mom would say I was making a mountain out of a molehill because I only had that one talk with Ethan and I don't know if he likes me at all in a boy-girl way. I had the feeling he did a little bit some of the time when we were talking, but I could have been imagining it. Like, even though he didn't say anything about my bikini, when we were talking he kind of glanced down at my breasts a few times, but just quickly, as though he didn't want me to notice. Maybe he feels the way I do: that if he liked me, Gretchen would hate it.

One other thing Gretchen said that time she got mad at me, was that I just wanted to add boys to my list of people who liked me, just to show off. She said I did that with Teddy, sort of stringing him along, even though I don't love him. It's true Gretchen would never go out with someone she just liked the way I like Teddy. She wants it to be true absolute love or nothing. She's very strict that way. I guess I'm more easygoing about it. I mean, I still hope to really love somebody at *some* point, but it might not be for years.

After Martin and I finished dinner, I said, "Did you ever like someone, only there was a reason you couldn't let them know about it?" Martin had been acting pretty nice, so I felt I could confide in him.

"Why couldn't they know about it?" he asked.

"Well, just for some reason. The reason doesn't matter. Did it ever happen to you?"

He thought a moment. "Well, I've liked girls who didn't like me back, if that's what you mean."

"No, not so much that they didn't *like* you as that—oh, I can't explain it."

"Why not tell me the real story and make it a little clearer?" he said, looking amused.

"In a way I'd like to tell you and in a way I wouldn't."

"Why?"

"Because now you're acting nice—but if you know

something and it's a secret, when you're not in a nice mood you'll probably start teasing me about it."

Martin laughed. "Am I so terrible?"

"Yeah, sometimes—like saying I'm too young to think this or do that. You're only nineteen months older than me, not a million."

"Listen, Ali, tell me or don't tell me. . . . Tess'll be over in a little while. Do you want some coffee?"

"Sure. Will you make it though?"

Martin stood up to clear the table with me and then got out the coffee pot, which is an electric one. "Should we have ice cream?" I said. "They have that chocolate chip kind."

"They used to. Tess and I polished it off this afternoon."

I looked and he was right. But there was still lots of coffee ice cream, which I like just as much, so I gave us each some. "It's Ethan," I said, "Gretchen's brother."

"*Him?*"

"Marty, come *on*. You promised you wouldn't tease me."

"I'm not. I just said, 'Him?' "

"It's the way you said it. I know you don't like him."

"I don't like him or not like him. We've spoken a few words to each other. He's not a friend of mine, but he seems okay."

"Gretchen really likes him," I said, speaking quickly. "I mean, they're really close, almost like best friends. They tell each other everything—at least she tells him everything."

"So, what exactly is your problem, my dear?" Martin

said, pulling the cord out of the coffee pot and talking in this pseudo low voice like a psychiatrist.

"It's that I know Gretchen would mind if she thought I liked him, but I can't help myself. I just keep thinking about him all the time, no matter what I do!"

Martin sighed. "A bad case. Grave."

"Marty, seriously. I wouldn't have told you if I thought you were going to make a big joke out of it."

"Look, she'll recover," he said.

"But will she still like me as a best friend?"

"Maybe not."

"Then what can I do?"

"If you want Gretchen as a best friend, concentrate on someone else. What's wrong with Teddy? He seems more your speed anyhow."

"Teddy's so—*I* don't know. Look, I've known him since I was five. I just don't *love* him and I don't think I ever will. By now I ought to know, don't you think? After nine years?"

"Give it another nine," Martin said, "and if, by then—"

"Martin, I'm never going to tell you *one* other single thing! I mean it!"

"Ali, you're taking a perfectly trivial thing and making a big deal about it."

I felt so mad. "What do you mean? Do you think you and Tess are trivial too?"

"That's completely different. This sounds from your account like a little crush that will blow over before you even finish thinking about it."

"Why should it? How can you tell?"

"I just can. Remember, we'll be back in New York in a month or so, and you won't even see him again for another year."

"True." That thought sobered me up. "Did you know with Tess right away, when you first met her, that you'd like her?"

"Well, partly, but it took a while till we really got to know each other."

Every time I speak to Martin about Tess, I keep thinking of that letter and I get embarrassed. Even his saying, "Till we really got to know each other" made me feel that way.

I went into the living room. I hate being alone in the house at night. I've always felt that way, ever since Mom stopped having baby-sitters. I hate that really empty feeling a house gets when you're alone. But it's babyish to talk about it, so I don't. Usually someone is home. It's pretty rare at home to have both Mom and Martin out on the same night. Martin doesn't mind being alone—he actually *likes* it! I know because I once asked him. He says that's the best time because it's so peaceful and quiet. One thing I do at times, which I know I shouldn't, is to turn the lights on all over the house. What I hate the most is going past a completely dark room. Sometimes I'll turn on just one light in every room, but if I feel *really* scared, I turn on practically every light! Then, when I go to bed, I turn some of them off. But once I forgot, and Mom practically hit the ceiling about what it would do to our electric bill.

"Will you be okay, Ali?" Martin asked as he was about to leave. When I was younger, sometimes, not often, but sometimes, one of Martin's dates would say, "Why don't we take her along?" and then I'd be in seventh heaven, gulping down huge bags of popcorn and watching some "grown-up" movie. But this time I knew he really didn't want me along, so I just said, "I'll be okay. I have a book I'm planning to read."

After Martin left, I thought I might watch TV, but there was nothing on. It's funny. I don't feel this way when I'm baby-sitting. I guess even having babies or children in the house makes me feel better, though I realize they couldn't do much if someone broke in. Anyway, I kind of moped around for a while and then decided to call Gretchen and see if she could come over for a few hours or maybe even sleep over. When I called, Ethan answered. "Oh hi," I said. "Is, um, Gretchen there?" I felt nervous after talking about him to Martin.

"She went to the movies with Mom."

"Oh . . . well, it was nothing special."

"Should she call you when she gets home?"

"Um . . . well, it doesn't really matter."

"You sound funny, Ali," he said. "Are you okay?"

"What do you mean?"

"Well, just nervous."

"Oh . . . yeah, well, I am, sort of, but for no good reason. It's just I'm here by myself. I thought I'd watch TV, but the movie they have is this really scary one, and

I'm afraid that would just make it worse."

"Would you like me to come over till someone gets home?"

My heart jumped. "Come over here?"

"If it would help."

"Yeah, well, sure, that would be terrific. But—"

"Okay, I'll see you in a little while."

After he hung up, I felt really excited. I began wishing that I'd washed my hair before supper and blown it dry and everything. For a second I wondered if I'd have time to do it before he came, but I figured I didn't. Anyway, he was only coming over because I said I was nervous. At least I didn't make it up. I mean, I really am nervous.

Ethan arrived about half an hour later. He looked nice. He had on a blue shirt and khaki pants. I wondered if he'd changed especially.

"I'm sorry," I said. "It's silly to be scared."

"No, I know how you feel."

"But you wouldn't feel that way, would you?"

"No, I like being alone—but everybody's different."

Now that he was here, I didn't know exactly what to do.

"If you want to watch that movie now that I'm here, why don't you?" he said.

"The scary one?"

"Yeah."

"No, I don't really like being scared. It's funny, most people do, but I really *hate* it. My heart starts beating too fast—it's just not a nice feeling. I can never figure out why some people like it." I knew I was babbling the way I always do when I'm nervous, but I couldn't stop myself.

"*We* had a mystery phone call tonight," Ethan said.

"The kind that says dirty things?"

"No. The kind that just sits there breathing into the phone and then hangs up."

"I'm glad we've never gotten *that* kind. That must be awful."

He sighed. "I think I know who it was," he said.

"You *do*?" I looked at him, puzzled.

"Well I have a pretty good idea."

"Who? How can you?"

"It's this guy. . . . Did Gretchen tell you we found out Mom was seeing this man, and they broke off when she and Roger got back together?"

I nodded. "You think it's him?"

"Yeah, I think so. He's done it some other times, and he hangs up whenever it's not Mom."

I didn't know what to say. "That must be awful."

"Well, I guess he still loves her or something."

"Does she love him?"

"I don't know. I guess she must have, once."

"Then why'd she go back to Roger?"

"Who knows? She's confused," he said wryly. He smiled. "Ali, the whole thing is such a mess. Your family is different. They seem relatively sane."

"Not always."

"Pretty much. Mom is just kind of—well, she never

knows *what* she wants to do about anything. Even little things. She changes her mind nine million times before she does anything. She'll probably have the baby and then decide she shouldn't have had it."

"Didn't she once see a psychiatrist?"

"Sure, she's tried everything. Yoga, est, you name it. She says she learns from all of them, but you'd never know it."

"You sound so detached about her."

Ethan frowned. "I guess that's my problem."

"Why is it a problem? I think it's *good* that you see her objectively. I don't think I do with my parents. I feel critical of Mom and Daddy sometimes, but I never know if it's me or them."

"I guess it's usually both."

"Yeah." Suddenly I felt ill at ease. "Do you want something to eat?" I said. "We have ice cream."

"Sure, why not?"

In the kitchen I kept thinking about how Martin had said my feelings for Ethan were trivial, and Teddy was more my "speed." I kept wondering why Ethan had come over. Did he know I liked him and did it mean he liked me, or did I just sound so desperate on the phone that he felt he had to?

"Do they leave you alone a lot?" Ethan asked, eating the ice cream.

"Uh uh. In New York, Martin hardly ever goes out, and Mom doesn't too much either. Sometimes she and Peggy go to a play or movie, but not too often."

"Does *your* mother have a boyfriend?"

"No."

"How come?"

"I don't think she's the type. I can't explain it exactly, but she doesn't seem to *want* one especially. I once tried to fix her up with this teacher from my school. I invited him over for dinner, but nothing much happened. She just said it was sweet of me to have thought of it. I mean, she doesn't talk about Daddy too much or why they didn't get along. *He* doesn't either."

"Why didn't they?"

"I don't know."

"Mom always grabs onto Gretchen and me and wants us to side with her about everything, just to have allies in the family." Ethan frowned. "If we don't, she gets hysterical and says she should never have had children and we don't love her, that kind of stuff. So naturally Gretchen feels sorry for her and tells her we really love her, and that makes her feel good for about three seconds."

"Don't *you* tell her that too?"

"Sometimes. But by now it's such a meaningless ritual, I hate to give her that satisfaction." He frowned again. "I don't even know if I *do* love her."

There was a pause.

"Would you like to go back into the living room?" I asked.

"Sure."

In the living room we sat side by side on the couch. I felt really attracted to him. He was sitting right next to me; our shoulders were touching. "Maybe I shouldn't have called you up," I said hesitantly.

"Why not?"

"Gretchen might not like it."

"I thought of that." He glanced at me and then away.

"The thing is," I said, not looking at him, "I'm afraid I might have a crush on you. I know it's stupid because I really don't *know* you that well."

"Oh," Ethan said. He looked embarrassed but pleased.

I felt glad I'd said it though. "Don't worry about it," I said. "You don't have to like me back or anything."

Ethan smiled. He took my hand. "I *do* like you, Ali."

"You don't have to say that."

"I know."

I looked at him and knew he was going to kiss me about three seconds before he did. Our faces moved closer and our lips touched. My mouth opened and he touched my tongue. When we pulled apart, he laughed nervously. "Wow."

"I'm so scared about Gretchen!" I said suddenly.

"We'll figure it out."

"If she started hating me, I couldn't *stand* it!"

"She won't hate you."

"She might. I'm afraid she might.

"Don't worry, Ali." He put his arms around me and we leaned back till we were lying down. Then we kissed some more. It was so different from kissing Teddy. Teddy is so nice looking, I love kissing him, but it never makes me that excited. With Ethan I felt like I didn't know what was going to happen next. I didn't even know what I *wanted* to happen.

"Maybe you should go home before they come back from the movie," I said. We were lying facing each other. His face was so close, our noses were touching.

He looked at his watch. It was ten thirty. "I think it gets out at eleven."

"You could still make it back. Would you, Ethan? Please?"

"Okay, but I don't think that solves anything in the long run."

"I'm going back to New York in a couple of weeks anyway."

"I know."

"So there is no long run, really."

"Is that what you're counting on?" he said.

I didn't know what to say. "I wish I could stay," I said softly.

"Could you?"

"How? Mom would have a fit."

He smiled. "Maybe she'd be glad to get rid of you."

"Uh uh . . . she wouldn't. Especially if I was going to stay with Daddy and Eileen. She'd hate it, I just know."

"Yeah, you're probably right. It's just some parents do that—shift the kids around from year to year."

"Mom said it would be bad for us, changing from school to school that way. And we're so far away that anything else wouldn't work. I wish we were really rich so we could fly back and forth all the time, for vacations and stuff."

Ethan stood up. He looked dazed. "I guess I better head back," he said. At the door he kissed me again. "Will you be okay? Don't be scared."

"I won't. I'm going to go to sleep anyway."

"Sweet dreams."

After he left, I didn't feel scared any more. I took a hot shower and washed my hair and, somehow, while I was drying it, I began feeling really tired. I fell asleep right away, before anyone came home.

Eight

The next day I kept thinking about Ethan. I'd start remembering our lying there, kissing, and then I'd imagine us taking our clothes off and doing everything. I think doing everything with Ethan would be really good. But that seems awful, wanting to when we've only been out on one date—not even a date.

At dinner Daddy and Eileen did most of the talking, so I don't think anyone noticed that I was sort of quiet. They were having a big salad with cold meat and other things mixed in. It tasted pretty good except for the avocado, which I never like.

While we were eating supper, the phone rang. I got up to answer it, but Eileen said, "I'll get it, Ali. Sit down and finish your dessert." Then, about a minute later, she said, "It's for you, Ali. It's a long-distance call."

I figured it must be Mom. I went over to the phone. "Hello?"

"Ali? Is that you? This is Peggy."

"Oh hi. I thought it'd be Mom."

"Well, it's Cynthia I'm calling about, actually. Now

listen, promise me you won't get upset, because Cynthia is feeling fine now, but the thing is, we were driving to Vermont yesterday and we had an accident with the car."

"What *kind* of accident?" I said, feeling my heart start to beat very fast.

"Well, we somehow slid off the road—it was raining —and smashed into some fenceposts. The car is a mess, but luckily neither of us was hurt too badly. Cynthia fractured some bones in her leg, and they're taking care of her in the hospital now."

"How come in the hospital," I asked, "if it's not serious?"

"It's serious in the sense that she needs medical care—her leg is in a cast—but it's not . . . there are no complications beyond that."

"Will she still be able to walk?"

"Oh sure. She can even get around now a little. It's just once the cast is off, she'll have to go for physical therapy for several weeks."

"Can—can I speak to her?" I was stammering, I was so nervous.

"Well, I'm not calling from the hospital. I'm back at our hotel, but I'll give you her number. Only Ali . . ."

"Yeah?"

"Don't call her right away. Wait till tomorrow. She's pretty tired and wrung out from the whole thing now. I think it's better if she gets a good night's sleep."

"Peggy, is she *really* okay? Are you really telling me the whole truth?"

"Definitely. Look, I even thought of not calling you till we were back in New York, but Cynthia felt you ought to know. Don't worry, Ali. I wouldn't lie to you about it."

"But you said the car got wrecked!"

"That can happen. Luckily, Cynthia had her seat belt on. And the car didn't actually turn over—it just crumpled in at the front."

"How will you get home?"

"We'll take the bus."

"Can I call her tomorrow?"

"Sure. She wants to speak to you, and Martin too, of course. Just tell him what I told you. But remember; no worrying."

"Okay," I said. "Thanks for calling, Peggy."

"Be well, Ali," she said.

I hung up. I still felt worried. I just couldn't see how a car could get all crumpled up like that and no one get hurt that much. I walked back into the dining room and sat down.

"What was *that* all about?" Daddy asked.

I swallowed and drank some water. My mouth felt all dry and funny. "It's about Mom. That was Peggy. She said they had a car accident. Mom's in the hospital."

"What?" Daddy looked startled. "What do you mean? Was she seriously hurt?"

"Uh uh. The car got all wrecked, but she's fine. I mean, something happened to her leg. She has a cast on it, but she can walk and everything. Peggy was sitting in the back, so she didn't get hurt."

94

"Who's Peggy?" Daddy said.

"Daddy, I *told* you. She's that woman who lives in our building—Mom's friend."

"Oh, you mean the one who . . . Cynthia stays with overnight?"

"Uh huh."

"Well, how did she happen to get mixed up in all this?"

"She said they were driving to Vermont."

"Why Vermont?"

"Daddy, I don't *know*. Mom knows someone in Vermont; I forget her name."

"So they're really that close?"

"Who?"

"Cynthia and this woman, Peggy?"

"What do you mean?"

"Well, I mean, taking vacations together and so on."

"I don't know. They're friends."

"Everything about this is odd," Daddy said. "Doesn't it strike you that way, Eileen?"

"We can talk about it later," Eileen said in a kind of tight voice.

Daddy looked at Martin, who had just been sitting there with a noncommittal expression. "What do you think, Marty?"

"They were going on a trip, the car crashed, what's the big deal? Nobody got hurt."

"True." Daddy was watching both of us.

I didn't see why he wasn't more worried about Mom being in the hospital. I always get scared when someone has to go to the hospital, even if it's for some minor thing. Seven years ago Mom had to go in to have one of her breasts tested for cancer. She didn't seem to mind that much and she was pretty cheerful, but I got really scared. This girl I used to be friendly with when I was in fourth grade, Sandra Magel, had open-heart surgery. She had to miss a lot of school. Whenever I'd come over to visit her, she'd keep talking about dying and being afraid her heart would never be the same. That got me scared because I can never figure out how things inside the body work, even when they're explained to me.

When Teddy came, I told him about Mom.

"Do you want to stay home and watch TV?" he asked.

I shook my head. "I just feel like being alone," I said.

Teddy looked puzzled. "Don't you want to try to get your mind off it?"

"I can't!"

"Maybe if we watched some show, you'd—"

"Teddy, I mean it! I don't *feel* like it! I just told you!" I didn't realize I was so upset till the words flew out of my mouth.

"Okay," Teddy said, looking hurt.

"I'm just not in the mood," I said. "Maybe tomorrow."

"I'll call you then," he said. He just stood there for a couple of seconds and then left.

I felt badly, but I knew that I didn't want to be with him. I can't talk about things like that with Teddy. I don't know why. But right then I didn't feel like talking to anyone that much. I just kept wishing I was home again. It wasn't that I didn't think Peggy was telling the truth, but still, I wanted to see Mom and make sure everything was okay. I kept wondering if what Peggy said about Mom's leg was true. Maybe it was something worse and she'd have to be in a wheelchair forever.

Daddy looked in the room and saw me sitting there. "I thought you were going out," he said.

"I'm not in the mood," I said.

"Because of Cynthia?"

I nodded.

"From what you said, it didn't sound that serious."

"But sometimes they just say that."

"You don't trust Peggy?"

"It's not that, but—"

"But what? Tell me, honey."

I looked down. "Well, that time Mom had to go into the hospital to have her breast operated on, checked, or whatever it was?"

"Yes?"

"Well, you lied to us then. You said she was going on a trip."

"That was because you were so young."

"I wasn't so young. I was seven."

"That's pretty young. Anyway, you may not remember this, but you were having some pretty bad nightmares around that time, and we were scared the truth would make it worse. Maybe we were wrong, but it was for a good reason."

"If I have children, I'll *never* lie to them about anything," I said fiercely.

97

"That'll be up to you. But I think when you're a parent, you'll see things from a slightly different perspective."

"No, I won't," I insisted.

"Ali, listen to me."

"I am."

"There's something I want to talk to you about."

"What is it?"

"This thing with Peggy and your mother. It has me concerned."

"How come?"

"I just sense something slightly peculiar about this relationship between them, this closeness."

"Why?"

"You don't see anything strange about it?"

"That they're friends? No, why should I?"

He looked embarrassed. "You don't think there's any chance that they, well, love each other?"

"You mean that they're gay?" I looked at him in amazement.

"Yes."

"Daddy, that's dumb. It's just ridiculous!"

"I hope so."

"Look, *everybody* has friends! So they go on some vacation together. How is that such a big deal?"

"Perhaps. Look, I may be reading between the lines," he said. "I admit that. But I have a funny feeling about it all."

"I think that's really crazy."

"Martin doesn't."

I frowned. "What?"

"He thinks there may be something to it."

"Why?"

"Because of various things. . . . It's something I want to look into and really get cleared up."

"Why don't you ask Mom?"

"Honey, come *on!* You don't think Cynthia would admit it to me, even if it were true?"

"Why shouldn't she?"

He hesitated. "She'd be afraid."

"How come? You wouldn't put her in *jail!*"

"No, but I might insist that you and Martin stay out here with me."

My heart started thumping. "Forever?"

"Till you're both in college."

"But Mom wouldn't like that. She wants us to be with her."

"It's up to a court to decide what environment is best for a child."

"We're not children!"

"Yes you are—and you especially, Ali. You're so vulnerable to everything. It could be a real disaster for you to stay under those circumstances."

"But what if I wanted to anyway?"

"It's not a matter of want. It's a matter of having someone who's in a position to be objective in deciding what would benefit you in the long run."

"Daddy, I'm fifteen! I'm not a baby! Anyway, what if she *is* gay? Lots of people are."

"I refuse to believe for a minute that you would be

that blasé about it if it proved to be true."

"I'm *not* blasé. I'm just not prejudiced. You always said we should judge people by what they're really like, not by outward things."

"Ali, listen, there are things about Cynthia that I've never told you about."

"Like what?"

"I'm not going to go into everything with you yet. I want to try and check this out."

"I think it's shitty."

"What?"

"Mom's in the hospital—she can't even *walk*, and you're plotting all these things behind her back."

"Not plotting. . . . Look, if it's true, wouldn't you want to know about it?"

"No, not especially," I said. That wasn't completely true, but I said it anyway. Whenever I argue with Daddy, he always wins by outtalking me, and I hate that.

"You'd rather hide from the truth than face it?"

"No!"

"That's what you just said."

"No, I mean, it's not that I don't want the truth, but if Mom wanted us to know, she'd have told us. She always tells us things."

"Ali, listen to me. There are certain things *I* know about that you don't. I mean, I do have a few years over you in age, and I've seen a little more of the world than you have. If you let me handle this, it can all work out for the best for everyone."

"What if I don't *want* to live here?"

"All of that is something we can't even go into now."

"Then why did you bring it up?"

"Because I happen to think it's important to get to the bottom of this. Would you rather I hadn't even mentioned it to you?"

"Yes!"

"Ali—"

"Daddy, it's not *fair!* She had this accident and everything. . . . So she has a friend! *I* have friends. You're making it all seem weird when it isn't."

"I've known Cynthia since she was nineteen years old. I'm not basing my opinion only on this incident you've told me about."

"If she's happy, why should you care?" I felt like I was going to cry. I bit my lip.

"I want what's best for you and Martin."

Daddy looked so threatening when he said that, I felt worse instead of better. I began to cry. "You don't, you don't."

"Ali, honey, look at you. This is what I mean. You've come out here all shaken up. I can see it—in your eyes, your voice, everything."

"That isn't true," I said, still crying.

"Every time Eileen makes any gesture of friendliness to you, you back off like it was some kind of attack. Where does that come from?"

"I *don't* back off!" I said. "I went shopping with her just a few days ago." I was breathing quickly. "I don't *want* to live with you and Eileen. I just *won't*. I don't care *what* you do!"

"No one is asking you to make that decision."

"So, what does it matter about Mom? She isn't going around poking into your life."

"You call it poking around to make it sound seedy. Look at Martin. Ever since he's come here, he's had a chip on his shoulder about Eileen. It's just as clear as day that Cynthia has been influencing the two of you against us."

"She hasn't," I said. "She doesn't even *care* about Eileen. She never even *talks* about her."

"Well, this didn't drop out of the bright blue sky."

"Eileen's not our mother. Why should we love her so much? *We* didn't marry her."

"Listen, Ali, maybe I was premature in even raising this whole thing. I thought you'd take it as a tribute to your maturity that I could talk to you about it. Evidently I was mistaken."

"Peggy's nice," I said.

"I'm sure Peggy's nice. That's irrelevant."

"You never even met her."

"Ali, you're somehow willfully missing the point. You're old enough to realize that raising children in a household with two homosexual women isn't exactly some kind of ideal. You're so emotional, honey. You *know* you are. What kind of feelings about men are you going to pick up living there? That's what concerns me. What kind of image will Martin have to base himself on?

It's one thing to have no father—how about two women who have decided to reject men absolutely?"

"They *haven't*," I said. "Daddy, you're wrong. Mom has friends who are men. She just doesn't want to get married again. What's so terrible about that?"

"Okay, Ali. Somehow, for some reason, you just want to misunderstand me. And I have to say I see that as part of this whole thing. You never used to be like this."

"How do you know?"

"What do you mean, how do I know?"

"You hardly even *saw* us except once a week. How do you *know* what I was like? Even Eileen said that."

"Said what?"

"That you were so, you know, absorbed in your work and all that."

For the first time in our conversation, Daddy looked uncertain. "Well, okay," he said, "there's some truth in that. But it doesn't mean I never noticed you or paid attention to you."

I sat staring at the carpet. It seemed like no matter what I said, he twisted it or turned it around or made it seem like he was only interested in my welfare. I hate it when adults do that.

"Do you believe I love you?" he asked suddenly.

I shrugged.

"That hurts me a lot, Ali. You know that, don't you?"

I looked down. I was scared I'd begin to cry.

"Honey, I want you to believe me when I say I love you very, very much. I wouldn't care in the least about

Cynthia or her sexual preferences or whatever if it wasn't for you. You have the potential to grow into a lovely, warm human being, and now I see how the whole thing could get horribly twisted. It scares me."

"If it's all not true, won't you feel stupid?" I said.

"Not in the least. I'll feel immensely relieved."

I sighed and lay back. "Daddy, I don't want to talk about this any more. Is that okay?"

"Of course it is."

He left me alone in the room. I really felt rotten. All I could think of was how awful Mom would feel if she found out—what a horrible fight this would lead to, almost like they were getting divorced all over again. I hate it when Daddy pretends everything is for my sake. I don't believe him any more. I just don't.

I started wondering if it *could* be true. It just doesn't seem possible to me. Mom and Peggy don't go around kissing each other or calling each other "darling" and stuff like that. You'd think, if what Dad said was true, they'd at least act a little that way, but they don't at all. Sometimes Mom makes sarcastic remarks about men, but she makes sarcastic remarks about a lot of things when she's in that kind of mood. Daddy does too, about women. Oh, I *hope* it's not true! I don't want a terrible fight. I don't want things to be different.

I tried to go to sleep, but I just couldn't. I lay there for around four hours, just thinking about everything. Finally, at about midnight, I went into the kitchen for a snack. I got out some raisins and cheddar cheese and sat at the kitchen table eating them. When I was almost finished, Martin came in in his pajamas.

"Hi," I whispered.

"Hi. Anything decent to eat?" He swung open the refrigerator door. Martin likes different things than I do for midnight snacks. He got out some chopped liver and spread it on a slice of pumpernickel bread.

"Marty?"

"Yeah?"

"Do you think it's true about Mom and Peggy?"

"Probably."

I stared at him. "Really? You think it's *true?* How come you never said anything about it?"

"I figured it was their business. I mean, if they wanted us to know about it, they'd have told us."

"But Mom *always* tells us things."

"Like Dad says, she was scared of losing us. Look, frankly, Ali, if it provides a way for us to live out here instead of going back, I'm for it."

"You'd really rather live here with Eileen and Daddy?"

"Sure."

I frowned. I guess if it had been even half a year ago or when we first left, I might almost have agreed. "I just think it's *mean*," I said. "If they want it to be private, Daddy shouldn't go poking around trying to find out things. Anyway, Mom's in the *hospital* and everything."

"She'll be out in a day or so. That's not important."

"But why do you think she got married if she was like that?"

"People change."

"Doesn't it seem strange to you? The idea of it?"

"In a way. But it seemed more strange when I first realized it."

"When was that?"

"Oh, months ago. Didn't you ever stop to think it was sort of odd their going off sleeping together in Peggy's apartment where there's only one bed?"

"I thought it was for us, to give us privacy." I stared at him intently. "Is that your only reason?"

"That was what made me start to wonder about it. But it was a lot of little things—the way they talk together, *I* don't know."

"But how come you didn't say anything?"

"To who?"

"To *me!*"

"Because I knew you'd get rattled. And it didn't seem relevant. It didn't occur to me to just take off for California. I thought we were stuck in New York for good, or at least till I went away to college. Do you wish I'd told you?"

"Sort of. I don't know."

He shrugged. "Maybe I should've. Listen, Ali, it might not even be true. I'm just guessing."

"Daddy scares me sometimes. He gets so determined about things. You'd really want to live here with him?"

"What's a place to live? It's just somewhere to set down your stuff. I want to be with Tess, and she's out here. I don't take it the way you do—as a question of loyalty to Mom. To me, it's just a practical thing."

"You mean, if it were the other way around, you'd stay with Mom? If it was her in California?"

"Sure."

Suddenly I felt really tired. I gave a big yawn. Except for being afraid I might have a bad dream, I really wanted to go to sleep. I put away the box of raisins and threw the empty cheese wrapper into the wastebasket.

Nine

In the morning everything was so much as usual that it seemed I just might have imagined the thing about Mom and Peggy. But then I found the piece of paper with Mom's phone number at the hospital on it, and it all came back to me.

I went to the phone in the living room since no one was in there. I even closed the door, because I wasn't sure who was up and who was sleeping.

On the phone Mom sounded just the same as usual. "Is your leg really okay?" I asked anxiously.

"Well, I can move around a little. Don't worry, darling. By the time you get home, I'll be back to normal. The doctor said I was really lucky."

"How did you do it?"

"I don't know. I was trying to change lanes, and somehow I swerved too far to the right. It was a crazy thing."

"You should have let Peggy drive."

"She'd been driving, but I was letting her rest for a while. Night driving scares me anyway."

"Mom? Do you, um, feel okay? I mean, apart from your legs?"

"I do. I really feel fine, darling. Promise me you won't worry."

"Okay."

"What's new out there? Are you still having a good time?"

I hesitated a second. "Pretty much."

"Why only pretty much?"

"No, things are good," I said.

"Sweetie, is anything wrong? You sound funny."

"I'm okay."

"Is Marty bothering you about anything?"

"Uh uh."

"Is it just something you don't want to talk about?"

I nodded and then remembered she couldn't see me. "Kind of." What I wanted was just to ask her about it point blank and have her laugh and say it was the silliest thing she'd ever heard.

"Sweetie?"

"Umm?"

"You know, if it's getting to be too much for you out there, why don't you come home early? Peggy and I are staying with friends at this lovely place in Vermont and we'll be here another ten days. You could just fly out here and then drive back to New York with us."

"With Marty too?"

"If he feels like it."

I thought a minute. "What kind of place is it?"

"It's just a kind of lodge. It's used for skiing in the

winter. Some women run it over the summer as a place for people to stay. There's swimming and tennis and a lot of stuff you'd really enjoy."

"I guess I better not," I said after a second.

"Look, don't, unless it's something that would be nice for you. I was afraid from the way you sounded that—well, I know how trying Eileen can be, and Harold isn't always the easiest person to be with."

"Yeah," I said, wanting to say more.

"I don't think they'd be hurt," Mom went on. "You've stuck it out this long. It's only a matter of a couple of weeks. And if you want an excuse, you could say—oh, I don't know—something about my accident or whatever. You don't have to be absolutely truthful."

"Sure."

"Think it over, Ali. Just remember it's there as an option."

"Okay, I will." It was *awful* wanting to tell her about the thing with Daddy but not being able to!

"It's been such a relief having Peggy here. I just got so panicked about the accident and she was as calm as could be."

"Uh huh."

"Should I call you when I come out of the hospital, sweetie? Let me give you the lodge number too, just in case."

I wrote it down on a piece of paper.

After I hung up, I just stood there for about five minutes, thinking about our conversation. Usually I tell Mom everything. I felt so awful and hypocritical not mentioning what Dad had said. But I was a little afraid she might say it was true. I didn't think she would, but I didn't want to take a chance.

Gretchen had asked me to sleep over at her house that evening. I went to pack my nightgown and toothbrush and stuff.

It had been hot lately, even at night sometimes, which is unusual out here—usually it cools off more at night. It's not half as bad as New York can be, but it's still pretty sultry. Daddy said there was a drought, and a lot of crops would be spoiled if it didn't rain soon.

As I was packing, I thought of how Ethan had asked me what I want to be when I grow up. Mom says it's never too soon to start thinking about that. But there's never any *one* special thing that I feel I want to do. Sometimes I've thought of being a lawyer like Daddy. It would be exciting to get up in a courtroom and argue a case. But what if you got nervous? I probably would, because I'm always nervous when I act in school plays.

I wonder if it's unrealistic to think of being a TV announcer. Everyone says I'm pretty and photogenic. I wouldn't have to think up things to say myself. They would probably hand me pieces of paper and I could memorize the lines. It would be exciting to be one of those people who sit at a table on election night and tell how many votes have come in from different states. I'd really like to have my own apartment in some place like New York. It wouldn't have to be too big, but I'd like it to have a terrace, and one of those refrigerators where you press a button and ice comes out, and a big, soft carpet so you could go around barefoot. I guess that *would* cost a lot of money. But announcers earn a lot. I read that somewhere.

Gretchen's mother and Roger were in the kitchen having lunch when I came over. They said Gretchen and Ethan were both out but would be back soon. "Have a seat, Ali," Gretchen's mother said. "Did you have lunch yet?" She was wearing denim shorts and a purple top that just covered her breasts like a strapless bra. Around her neck was a silver pig on a chain.

"Well, I had sort of a late breakfast," I said. It was the first time Gretchen's mother had looked at all pregnant to me. Right in front her belly swelled out a little.

"How about some coffee or soda?"

"Soda would be fine."

I wish Gretchen hadn't told me about her mother's affair. Now every time I'm with her I feel uncomfortable. I guess I can't figure out exactly why she decided to get back together with Roger again. Roger was eating a sandwich and not talking much, as usual. He's tall and thin with shaggy blond hair. He's a stage manager.

"Gretchen will certainly miss you when you go back to New York, Ali," Gretchen's mother said. She was eating cherries and had the pits arranged like a face on her plate.

"I'll miss *her* too," I said.

"It's such a *pity* you had to go that far, all the way across the country."

"Yeah, I wish it could've been somewhere out here."

"But I guess with jobs so hard to get nowadays, you go where you can find them."

Roger looked up at me. He likes me, I can tell. "Cynthia's happy with her new job?" he asked.

"I guess." I wasn't sure Mom was so happy with it, but she certainly was busy.

"You know, Ali," Gretchen's mother said, "I was hoping that when you left, Gretchen would make some new friends at school. It's *pathetic* how isolated she is in a school that big! She doesn't even *try!* All she does is talk to Ethan! She *uses* him like a shield from the outside world. What's she going to do when she's out in the world? She can't hang on to him forever."

"Well, I guess she won't," I said, not knowing what to say.

"*Why* do you think she's like that?" Gretchen's mother asked in that intense way she has. Her long, thin fingers touched my arm. "*I* was shy as a girl—you might not know it from the way I am now. Not in this extreme way Gretchen is, but—and she's pretty, don't you think?"

"Yes, I do," I said, feeling uncomfortable.

"She's not *sexy* looking or—you know—but she could be pretty if she made an effort. A little makeup. *Something*. But then look at Ethan! He's hardly any better, always burying himself in a book. I can't talk to either of them! If I ask Gretchen about it, she says she'd rather not talk about it. She's so sensitive! I just want to help her. Is that so terrible?" She bit her lip, frowning.

I shook my head.

"I want to tell her I *care*. Isn't it ironic? When I was young, all I wanted was to know my mother cared or was interested in what was happening to me. And she wasn't. Not in the least. I'd have been so *flattered* if she'd come to me when I was Gretchen's age and said, 'Honey, is there something bothering you?' I'd have been the happiest girl you can imagine." She looked pensive. Gretchen's mother has beautiful eyes with really long eyelashes. "Well, maybe the baby will change all that."

"Your baby?"

"Hasn't Gretchen told you?" She pointed to her stomach with a smile. "Yes, it'll be late in the fall, October or November, probably. I'm just beginning to feel it. At first it was a shock to her, but I think she's taking to the idea a little bit more now. It could be a new thing for her, you know? Something to focus on outside herself. It's this self-absorption that's so bad for her."

Roger smiled. "She'll like the baby, Terry. Don't worry."

"I *think* so." But she still looked uncertain. "It's just with Gretchen you simply can't *tell*. Ali, what do *you* think about this thing with Ethan? Don't you think it's unhealthy? *My* brother and I used to fight like cats and dogs!"

"I think it's nice they're friendly," I said cautiously.

"I wouldn't mind it so much," Gretchen's mother said, "if there was some boy in the picture. Anyone! Tall, short, fat, thin: just a boy—that's all I ask."

"She has plenty of time for that later," Roger said.

"Later! Sure, when she's forty?" She took the silver pig in her hand and held it, rubbing it back and forth. Roger was watching her.

There was a pause. I kept praying Gretchen would come back. I remember Mom used to say that Gretchen's mother could "chew your ear off." That seemed like a really appropriate expression.

"How about that boy *you* were seeing, Ali? How's he?"

"Teddy?"

"Yes, he seemed like *such* a darling. Why can't Gretchen find someone like that?"

"I guess her taste is different than mine," I said.

"She'll find someone when she's in college," Roger said.

"Will she?"

"I think older men will like her."

Gretchen's mother suddenly looked hopeful. "That's true. In college a lot of girls come out of their shells. Maybe Gretchen will too. What do *you* think, Ali?"

"Sure," I said, just to say something. "I think she'll meet somebody in college."

She leaned forward intently. "You don't ever—your Teddy doesn't have a friend by any chance? I was just thinking the four of you, if he has one, might, you know, do something together because Gretchen feels so much more comfortable with you around."

"I'll ask him," I said, knowing how much both Teddy and Gretchen would hate the idea.

"It doesn't have to be a big romance, something where

they're matched together by computer—just a boy, someone friendly, nice relaxed, *you* know what I mean."

"Okay," I said.

"You're a sweetheart." She smiled at Roger. "Isn't she darling, Roger? You've gotten so *pretty* these past few years, Ali. How did it happen so fast? Look at you!"

I blushed. They were both staring at me.

"Your figure, everything—and you dress so nicely. I just wish Gretchen would—"

"Terry, lay off Gretchen, will you?" Roger said. But he reached out and put his hand on her shoulder.

"She just doesn't take advantage of what she's got," Gretchen's mother said plaintively. "And if she doesn't, who will? Who'll know?"

Roger sighed and smiled at me, as though realizing there was no getting through to her. "So, how's New York?" he said, getting up to put away the rest of his sandwich. "Are you settling in? I used to live there—on East Twelfth Street."

"It's good," I said. "I like it."

"I felt so sorry for Cynthia when she had to move out there with the two of you—and Harold three thousand miles away," Gretchen's mother said. She got up and began clearing plates. "The courage! *I* couldn't do it—I know that—pulling up roots that way."

"Well, jobs in her field are hard to get," Roger said. He was looking at Gretchen's mother as she bent to pick up the plates. The silver pig swung down and clinked against a glass.

"True. What're you thinking of doing when you get out of college, Ali?"

"I'm not sure yet."

"You used to draw lovely pictures. Do you remember, Rog?"

"They were beautiful," Roger said.

"You might be an artist," Gretchen's mother suggested. "Have you given any thought to that?"

"Sometimes."

"I still remember that one you did of Gretchen. It caught her likeness perfectly."

Just then Gretchen came riding up on her bike. When she saw me in the kitchen with her mother and Roger, she scowled. "How come you came so early?"

"I just felt like it."

"Come on into my room," she said.

"Where's the hello?" Gretchen's mother said wryly.

"Hello," Gretchen muttered.

When we were in Gretchen's room, she said, "I bet she was telling you to fix me up with some freak or something."

"No," I said. I was too embarrassed to tell Gretchen all her mother had said.

"*Her* life is such a mess, but she keeps trying to run mine!" Gretchen said, flopping down on the bed.

"She said she hopes you'll like the baby once it comes."

"And if I don't, she'll say how weird I am, not to be like everyone else. That's *all* she wants—for me to be like everyone else. She's such a conformist."

"Roger is nice though."

"Yeah," Gretchen said in a soft voice. "But he never stands up to her."

"I guess he loves her."

Gretchen looked at me a moment without answering. "I guess," she said finally.

Ten

Gretchen's mother and Roger went out for supper. That meant we had the whole house to ourselves. Ethan was off somewhere. I kept wondering if I should tell Gretchen about his coming over to see me, the way I would have if he hadn't been her brother, but I couldn't.

We fixed some spaghetti. Gretchen made this special sauce for it out of an egg yolk and some heavy cream with Parmesan cheese all mixed in. It was really great. We ate it from gigantic orange soup bowls.

"Mom was in a car accident," I said while we were eating.

"Really? What kind? Was it serious?"

"Uh uh. She was driving somewhere and ran into some posts. The car got all crumpled up evidently."

"How scary! Is she okay?"

"Pretty much. She has a cast on her leg, but she'll be out of the hospital pretty soon."

Gretchen still looked worried. She hates hearing about death or sickness even more than I do. "What if she'd been killed?" she said.

"I know."

"What would you have done?"

"I don't know. I guess I'd have had to live with Daddy and Eileen."

"Would you want to?"

"Not so much, I guess. Daddy would like it though."

"How come?"

"He just thinks it would be good," I said, unable to tell her the truth. "He misses us, I guess."

"I thought you said he never paid that much attention to you when you were little."

"Maybe that's why, to make up for it, or maybe we seem more interesting now."

"I just wish you didn't live so far away!"

"Me too." I wanted to bring up the thing about Mom and Peggy, but I didn't know how. "Do they have this gay lib thing out here?" I asked.

"What do you mean?"

"Like in the papers and stuff? Where we live, they have a special newspaper just for people who are gay."

"Maybe they have one here too," Gretchen said. "I don't know."

"I wonder what they're like, gay people."

"Weird, I guess."

"Do you think they're *all* weird?"

"I don't know. No, maybe that wasn't so nice to say. I mean, who knows? But some of them seem kind of far out."

"I read this article that said everyone is partly man and partly woman, so everyone is really a little gay."

"I don't know if I believe that," Gretchen said.

"Me neither," I said hastily. "I just read it someplace."

"There was a gay woman Mom was friendly with who was in a play with her. She seemed pretty regular. I mean she didn't *act* that strange the times I saw her."

"Was she married?"

"Yeah. She had a kid too. Some of them are married. I mean, I guess they start off liking men, but they change their minds, maybe because they have a bad experience or something."

"You mean if they had a good experience it wouldn't happen?"

"*I* don't know. Maybe." Gretchen set down the dishtowel. "Let's see what's on TV," she said.

I followed her into the living room. We found some old movie that wasn't so good, but we watched it anyway. At around eleven we decided to go to sleep. Ethan still wasn't home. In a way I was glad, because I knew I'd feel uncomfortable with him if Gretchen was there. At the same time, I wondered where he was. I had looked forward to seeing him, so I was a bit disappointed when he didn't show up. As we were getting undressed for bed, I asked, "Where's Ethan?"

"I don't know," Gretchen said, "At a movie or visiting someone, I guess."

Gretchen had a trundle bed in her room which pulled out from under her own bed. We fixed it up with these really pretty sheets. "Do you want a blanket?" she asked.

I shook my head. "It's too hot."

"I don't think I'll even wear pajamas," Gretchen said. "Maybe just underpants."

"Me too."

We got into bed and talked a little bit after the light was out.

"Have you been seeing Teddy much?" Gretchen asked.

"Not *so* much." I told her how I'd gotten mad at him the night I found out about Mom's accident. I still felt a little guilty about that.

"Do you let him kiss you?"

"Usually."

"How is it?"

"It's good. He's a good kisser."

"What do you mean?"

"I don't know, he's just good." Sometimes I wish Gretchen had at least some experience so she would know what I was talking about.

"Do you let him put his tongue in your mouth and stuff like that?"

"Sometimes."

"That always sounds so yucky to me."

"It's sort of nice," I said hesitantly.

"Isn't it all *wet* though?"

"Yeah, but, well, I can't explain it."

Gretchen was silent for a while. Then she said, "Sleep well, Ali."

"You too."

Gretchen's house is off the main road, so it was

really quiet. You don't hear cars passing as much as you do at Daddy and Eileen's house. But I just couldn't get to sleep. I kept thinking about Ethan and wishing he'd come home. I turned around a lot, trying to find a comfortable position. I looked over at Gretchen. She was sprawled out with the sheet just up to her knees and her pillow scrunched to one side. Her breasts are really small when she lies on her back like that. Then I started thinking about Mom and Peggy again and if what Daddy thought about them was true. I thought of them lying naked together, and touching each other, and calling each other "darling" and "sweetie." But it was hard to imagine. I could imagine them loving each other because I love Gretchen, but I just couldn't imagine the physical part so much. Like I couldn't imagine Gretchen and me suddenly touching each other or kissing each other, even when we were sleeping without our clothes. It's not that it would be bad. I just didn't know if I'd really want to do it that much.

I closed my eyes. I began just lightly touching my body, pretending it was Ethan's hand touching me. I ran my hand over my breasts. When I did it, my nipples got smaller; then sort of shrunk. I let my hand go down my belly and then slowly around inside my thighs. The skin there is so soft!

I thought of Daddy and Eileen, and Gretchen's mother and Roger. Daddy and Eileen have separate beds, side by side, but Gretchen's mother and Roger have one big bed that takes up almost the whole room. When I get married I want to have one big bed. I think it must be nice to snuggle up with someone, not just for sex but to feel them next to you when you fall asleep.

I guess I finally dozed off, because it seemed a long time later when Gretchen was yanking my arm and saying, "Do you want to come?"

"What?" I yawned.

"Ethan's back. We're going for a swim."

I looked up groggily and saw Ethan in the doorway. I felt kind of embarrassed because I had nothing on except underpants. Still, it was pretty dark and the sheet covered me a little. I pulled it all the way up to my neck. "What time is it?"

"Two," Gretchen whispered. "Don't make a lot of noise though. Mom and Roger are home."

"Okay," I whispered.

When Ethan left the room, I rummaged in my bag for my bathing suit. Suddenly I didn't feel at all sleepy.

Outside it was nice, not as hot as it had felt in the room. We splashed around, but quietly so they wouldn't hear us. They don't have a regular light for the pool, just one for the outside of the house, so you have to be careful when you get in.

Afterward we sat on the grass. "I'm thirsty," Gretchen said.

"What do you want?" Ethan asked. "I can get it."

"I don't know. What *is* there?"

"Just milk and that drink they mixed for the party, sangria."

"The stuff with the oranges and lemons in it?"

"Yeah."

"Oh. Is it good?"

"We can try it."

Ethan brought the pitcher of sangria outside along with three plastic cups. I tasted mine first. "Hey, it's really *good*," I said. "It's not like real wine at all."

"It has a lot of orange juice in it," Gretchen said. "I saw her make it."

"Better look out, kids," Ethan said. "It's stronger than it seems."

"It can't be if it's mostly orange juice," Gretchen said.

"I think it has brandy too."

We sat there drinking and talking. "We should have slept outside," Gretchen said. "It's so much cooler here."

"Umm." I lay down on the grass. "We still could."

Gretchen yawned. "We'd have to get up so early then, when the sun came up." She held out her glass. "Is there any more of that stuff?"

"This is the end," Ethan said.

"Will they mind that we drank it?" I asked.

"No, it was just left over," Gretchen said. A few minutes later she rolled over on her stomach and about a minute later started to snore. It wasn't really loud snoring, more that kind of heavy breathing people do when they're asleep. I looked at Ethan. He smiled at me. I got that funny feeling in my stomach. I thought of how I'd touched my body, pretending it was him touching me. I was glad he didn't know I'd done that.

"I guess she had a little too much," he said softly.

"What should we do with her?"

"I don't know. Let her sleep, I guess. I think I might go in for another swim."

"Okay, I will too."

We swam around in the dark, passing each other silently. It felt safe in the water, cool and quiet. I kept thinking Gretchen might wake up, but she didn't.

"I think we'd better carry her inside," Ethan said when we got out.

"How?"

"You take her feet and I'll take the rest of her."

Actually Gretchen is very light—she only weighs a hundred pounds. She didn't even seem to notice us lifting her up. We carried her into the bedroom. I put a towel under her in case her suit was still wet. Then I pulled the sheet over her.

"So, mission accomplished," Ethan said. He smiled at me again in that special way.

"She must really sleep soundly," I said. "I'd have woken up."

We went out in the hall, still keeping our voices low.

"I better bring the sangria and glasses in," Ethan said, "or I'll get it in the morning."

Together we fixed things up pretty much the way they'd been. I couldn't tell if it was because I was drunk or not, but I felt peppy and excited all of a sudden. "Are you going to go back to sleep?" I said.

"Are you?"

I shrugged. "I don't know. I don't feel like it."

"Come into my room and we can talk."

"Okay."

My suit was still wet so I changed into my nightgown before I went into Ethan's room. I was glad I'd brought a pretty one. It's lavender with a ruffle in front. Ethan had changed into pajamas too. They had blue and white stripes. I sat down on the floor. All of a sudden I felt uncomfortable, maybe because we were together in his room.

"I hope Gretchen doesn't wake up," I whispered.

"Don't worry." He sat down next to me. We were both leaning against the back of his bed.

"Where were you before?" I asked.

"I just went for a walk."

"By yourself?"

"Yeah."

"How come you didn't go with anyone?"

"I like being alone."

"Don't you like to talk about things while you're walking?"

"Sometimes. . . . Ali?"

"Yeah?"

"Can I kiss you?"

"Sure," I said breathlessly.

Ethan leaned forward and put his hands on my shoulders. My hair was still damp. I could feel a few drops trickling down my neck. We kissed and stopped and kissed again. His hand was shaking slightly. "Ali?"

"Yeah?"

"What do you want to do?"

"I don't know."

He hesitated. "How does this unfasten?" he asked, touching the top of my nightgown.

"Like this." I undid the button at the neck and pulled my nightgown over my head. I still had on my bikini underpants.

Ethan looked at me for a long time. "You're *so* pretty, Ali."

"Thank you." I swallowed. I felt nervous, having him look at me that way.

He reached out and touched my breasts.

"Your hands are so cold!" I said, shivering.

"I guess I feel nervous."

"Me too."

"Do you want to—should we lie down on the bed?"

"Okay."

Ethan laughed.

"What's so funny?"

"I was expecting a lot of resistance."

I didn't know what to say. "I guess I trust you."

He took off his pajama top. We lay close together, facing each other. His skin was cool all over from swimming. I could feel his heart pounding. We kissed again slowly. We turned around kissing, tangled together. He was lying almost on top of me.

Suddenly he drew in his breath. "Oh, Ali, I—"

"What?"

"I'm going to come, I can't—" I felt his body jerk against mine. Afterwards he held me in his arms. "I'm sorry," he said.

"It's not your fault."

"I just couldn't hold back."

"That's okay. I don't mind." I looked up at him. "Did you, um, ever . . ."

"No." He smiled. "Did you?"

"Uh uh. This is the most I ever did."

He hestitated. "Are you still seeing that guy?"

"Teddy? A little."

"You said you didn't like him that much."

"Well, he's like an old friend. I don't see him a *lot*."

"I don't get it," Ethan said. He sounded hurt and angry.

"Get what?"

"Look, Ali, maybe it's *me* who's strange, but I would think if you, well, if you're interested in one guy, you wouldn't keep stringing another one along."

"I don't like Teddy the way I like you," I said, my lips pressed against his chest. "I never did. I was never in love with him." I stopped. I guess you're not supposed to tell a boy you love him till he tells *you*, but I *do* love Ethan, so why shouldn't he know?

He looked down. "I wish so much you could stay out here all year!" he said intensely.

"Me too."

I stayed in his room for a long time after that. We lay in each other's arms and talked and talked. I told him all about Mom and what Daddy had said. And he told me lots of things about himself. I felt good to have Ethan talk to me about personal things, because I knew he wasn't the kind of person who would say those things to just anyone.

Finally, we both began yawning. I knew we'd been lying there a long time, but I had no idea what time it was. "I guess we better go to sleep," I said. "It's almost morning."

"It *is* morning," Ethan said, getting up to look at his clock. It was five o'clock. He smiled at me. I smiled back. We stood there, beaming at each other in a kind of dopey way. Then he hugged me tight. "Sleep well, Ali."

When I got back into bed I couldn't get to sleep, even though I was really tired. I felt so excited, sort of light, as if I was filled with helium, like those balloons that go up in the trees if you let go of the string. Looking over at Gretchen, I felt a pang. *Don't mind*, I prayed silently, looking at her. *Please don't mind, Gretch.*

Eleven

I slept till almost noon. When I woke up, light was streaming through the venetian blinds. I looked over at the other bed, but Gretchen wasn't in it. Then I remembered everything—the swimming, the sangria, Ethan. I brushed my teeth slowly and started getting dressed. I was in my bra and jeans when Gretchen came in. I smiled. "Hi!" I said, maybe too cheerfully.

"Hi," Gretchen said in a very downbeat way.

"Um, when did you get up?" I asked, pulling a T-shirt over my head.

"At nine," she said curtly.

"I'm sorry I slept so late, Gretch. I was so tired. It must have been the sangria."

"You only had one glass."

"I guess alcohol makes me sleepy. Anyway, *you* should talk! You fell asleep on the lawn. We had to *carry* you in!"

I thought Gretchen would say, "Did I really?" or be surprised the way people in movies are on the morning after. But she just turned away and began pulling at the sheet on her bed. "Did you have breakfast yet?" I asked hesitantly.

"I *told* you I got up at nine!"

I stood there awkwardly for a second and then said, "I guess I'll fix myself something then." I wanted to add, "Is Ethan up?" but I figured I'd see him if he was, so I didn't ask.

In the kitchen some coffee was on. Gretchen's mother was cooking hamburgers. She was wearing a short turquoise-blue, terrycloth robe, belted around her waist. "Hi, Ali," she said. "Can I fix you one?"

"I better have something more like breakfast," I said. I looked in the cupboard where Gretchen's mother keeps the cereal and got down a box of Product 19. Then I sat down at the table and began eating.

"Where's Gretchen?" her mother asked.

"I guess she's in her room."

"You two must have been up half the night talking! Well, I guess you still have a lot to catch up on."

"Sort of," I said. I began mushing up the cereal. "Is Ethan up?"

"No, not a peep out of him."

Just as I was scraping some of my leftover cereal into the garbage, Ethan walked in. "Hi," he said. He smiled at me, a special smile.

I smiled back, feeling happy again, despite Gretchen.

"Hamburgers!" he said, peering into the pan.

"It's noon, my dear," his mother said. "There are those of us who awakened some time ago."

"Wow, I'd better get going," he said. "My tutoring lesson is at one."

I didn't know what to do. I sat there watching Ethan pour himself some coffee. A minute or two later Gretchen came in. She reached for a pair of scissors on the pegboard and then walked out again without saying anything. I was beginning to get a nervous feeling about the way she was acting.

Mostly out of cowardice I stayed in the kitchen till it was time for Ethan to leave. We couldn't talk much since his mother was there. Then, reluctantly, I went back into the bedroom.

Gretchen was on the floor, cutting something out of felt.

"What's that?"

"Just a design," she said, not looking up.

"Ethan went to his tutoring lesson," I said, just to say something.

"I know," Gretchen said.

I sat down and swallowed a couple of times before I said, "Is something wrong, Gretch?"

"Oh, cut it out, Ali."

"Cut what out?"

"*You* know what happened."

"I don't!"

"Well, just think about it for a few seconds."

"About what?"

"About last night."

"You mean, our going swimming and the sangria? Did your mother get mad?"

"You have a hundred guesses."

"Why don't you just tell me?"

"I want you to guess."

"Gretch, please! Just tell me what it is."

"It's about you and Ethan," she said, staring off in the corner.

My heart began thumping. "What *about* us?"

"I wasn't asleep last night," she said.

"You mean, when we carried you inside?"

"Right." She looked up at me. "What happened after you carried me in?"

"Well, I, uh, went to sleep."

"You did not! You went into Ethan's room and stayed there till five o'clock!"

"Were you awake that whole time?" I said incredulously.

"Yes!" she said. "Even *after* five o'clock." She glared at me. "I feel like killing myself!"

"Gretch, we were just *talking*," I said softly. I felt so terrible.

"Sure. That's why you had the door closed, I guess."

"We just closed it because we didn't want to wake anyone up."

"Ali, you're lying! Stop it! I *hate* that. I hate it worse than whatever else happened."

I didn't know what to say. "It just—we really didn't do that much," I stammered. "It really was mostly talking."

"I know all about your idea of nothing much! Tongue kissing and all the rest of it."

"Gretch, I'm sorry. Really."

"Well, *I'm* not! I'm glad I found out. There's probably more I don't even know about. Stuff you've done behind my back."

I thought of the night Ethan had come over when I was scared. "No," I said.

"I'm never going to trust one single person again in my whole life," Gretchen said.

"Gretch, we weren't . . . we both still, you know, love you."

"The way you love each other?"

"It's different, but . . ." I knelt down beside her on the rug. "You're still my best friend," I said, "out of everyone."

"Stop it, Ali!"

"It's true. If I didn't have you to talk to, I'd go crazy."

"Why? Now you have Ethan."

"It's different though."

"Yeah, it's great for you. Now you have two people and I have none."

"Do you want me to never see him again? Look, I'm going back to New York in two weeks anyway."

"You'll probably write to him."

"Would you mind that?"

"Yes!"

I didn't know what else to say. "That's not fair."

Gretchen didn't answer.

I decided to go home. I put my nightgown into the bag I'd brought and went to get my toothbrush and toothpaste out of the bathroom.

Gretchen's mother looked in. "Another hot day, girls. Don't stay in the sun too much."

Gretchen didn't say anything. I tried to smile. "I guess I'd better . . . I told Eileen I'd be back by lunchtime."

"Oh, what a pity," Gretchen's mother said. "Well, I know you'll be back soon, Ali."

Gretchen didn't say one single word as I packed. She just sat there, sort of hunched over, drawing something on the rug with her finger.

"Well, so long," I said when I was done. She still didn't look up.

Walking home, I felt awful. If only Ethan wasn't Gretchen's brother! But then I'd probably never have gotten to know him or maybe, if I'd met him just once or twice, I wouldn't have liked him. It just isn't fair. He's her *brother*, not her boyfriend. But the trouble is, I knew how Gretchen felt about Ethan. Then I thought again of being in his room, talking, kissing, lying there. I *couldn't* not see him again! Maybe after a day or two Gretchen will feel better. Maybe it wasn't what we did so much as our doing it behind her back. I once read somewhere that betraying a trust is what people mind most. Only *she* was doing something bad by letting us think she was asleep. That was sneaky, trying to trap me. She'd acted just like she was asleep, lolling her head over, breathing that way.

When I got back to Eileen and Daddy's house, no one was there. It was still early afternoon. I felt sort of sleepy, even though I'd gotten up at noon. Sometimes, if there's something I'm worried about, I just go to sleep so

I won't have to think about it anymore. That's sort of cowardly, I guess. I got into bed without anything on. Rolling over, I pressed a blanket between my legs. At first I pretended it was Ethan making love to me, but in the end it got all blurry in my mind. It was like it was partly Ethan and partly that man I sometimes think of who was in *Playgirl* and partly no special person, just a feeling. Right afterwards, I fell asleep and didn't dream about anything at all.

Twelve

"Ali?"

It was Daddy. I sat up, sleepily.

"It's five o'clock," he said. "We'll be having supper soon."

"Oh. Okay." I would have gotten out of bed except I didn't have anything on.

"Can I talk to you for a minute?"

"Sure. Could you wait just one second?" I wrapped the sheet around me, ran over to the closet, and put on my bathrobe. It's this old plaid one that I've had for about three years, but it still fits.

Daddy came over and sat on the edge of the bed. I sat down cross-legged on the floor, looking up at him. "Actually, it's really just . . . I wondered if you'd given much thought to what we talked about."

"You mean about Mom?"

"Yes, but more particularly what I mentioned to you about where you want to live next year."

"Well, it's just that Mom would feel terrible if I didn't go back."

"Darling, please focus totally on where *you* want to live. That's the only thing that counts."

I thought of how I wouldn't see Ethan again for a long time if I went back to New York, maybe a year. And I knew it would take longer than the time I had left to make up with Gretchen. "Well, in some ways I'd like to stay here," I admitted, "but—"

Daddy smiled. He put out his hand and ruffled my hair. "I'm so glad, sweetheart. You don't *know* how happy that makes me."

I held back. "It's not because of those things you said about Mom and Peggy though."

"That doesn't matter. Look, sweetheart, I'm a lawyer, so please just trust in me and leave the legal part of it up to me. What we care about now is implementing what you and Marty want. That's all. If it happens that anything about Cynthia and her friend is relevant——which I think it is—it will have to come up."

"But Daddy, I need more time to think it over."

"Of course. But will you promise me that if we go to court, you'll tell the judge everything openly and frankly, everything you've told me?"

"Like what?" I looked at him, worried.

"Like that evening you were left alone."

"I wasn't alone."

"Well, you know the incident I mean—when Cynthia went off with her friend. You just describe what happened. The judge will weed through all the problems and come up with a solution."

I was silent a minute. The thought of going to court

and talking to the judge scared me. "Would I go to the same school as before," I asked, "if I stay?"

"Sure. Unless you'd rather not."

"I'd like to be with my friends again."

"Of course!" Daddy leaned forward intently. "You see, Cynthia's decision—to take you two so far away—was very, *very* irresponsible. I don't like to say this to you, but in many ways she is *not* responsible. I should have prevented it."

"How?"

"I don't *know*. I should have insisted you both stay here with me." He frowned. "I really think this will be good for Cynthia. Let her realize how painful that move was for me. She never thought of that!"

I sighed. I felt all funny inside. "Daddy, I feel all mixed-up about this. I'm so worried about Mom. I think she might really be upset if I stay."

"She'll accept it. She doesn't *have* to like it. She has to take the responsibility for her actions or her life style or whatever you want to call it."

"Does Eileen want us to stay?"

"Of course she does! I've been trying to tell you that all summer. Eileen is crazy about you two. All she wants is for you to give her a chance. No, sweetheart, the real thing is I want you and Marty to experience what a happy home is like. You deserve that."

"Mom is happy."

"Okay. I should have said a normal, average, typical family."

I sighed. I went over and put my arms around him. "Oh, Daddy!"

"What, honey?" He held me close, stroking my hair. It felt good.

"If only I hadn't started liking Ethan!"

He frowned. "Who's Ethan? What has *that* got to do with this?"

"He's Gretchen's brother and, well, I started to like him and I don't want to move away just when we've started to like each other."

"That's perfectly natural," Daddy said.

"But Gretchen doesn't like it."

"Oh well, she'll learn to handle it."

"Maybe."

"That alone, I admit, would hardly constitute a reason for your staying here," he said. "But it adds to the total picture and that's what we have to keep in mind—the total picture."

I pulled away enough to look up at him. "If you wanted us so much, how come you didn't get joint custody?"

Daddy looked embarrassed. Then, as though pulling himself together he said, "I felt . . . well, Eileen and I hadn't been married so long. I wasn't sure how our relationship would turn out . . . all those things."

"*Is* it turning out?"

"Yes, I think so. I mean, we sometimes disagree, like anyone else, but that's natural."

"But Daddy?"

"Yes?"

"If Mom is gay, how come you married her?"

He looked reflective. "She wasn't when I married her. I mean, she had these rather intense friendships with women, but I never felt . . . . She did have this one friend, Ann, who used to come over all the time and always seemed terribly resentful of me. But I only wondered if there might be something on Ann's side. I never thought Cynthia . . . I remember once I came home and there was Ann, sobbing her heart out about something, and Cynthia was stroking her head and murmuring comforting things. But when I said something about it, Cynthia got furious and accused me of reading all sorts of things into it."

"So you, like, really loved each other—for a while anyway?" I asked.

He looked sad. "Yes, for a while we certainly did. For a long while."

"Do you mind about Mom and Peggy though?"

"Well, I mind to the extent it influences both of you. Otherwise, obviously, it's her decision."

"No, but I mean, do you think there's anything wrong with it?"

"Yes, I suppose in a way I do."

"*I* don't."

"Okay, that's perfectly fine. You think whatever you like, Ali. I could say you're a little young to have really well-founded opinions on something like this, but that's another story."

"Would I have to tell the judge I minded?"

"Not really. I mean, we *will* have to go over what you say to him. I don't think he'll question you point blank on that. It doesn't really matter. The evidence speaks for itself."

"What do you mean?"

"I mean, most judges, most people, would agree that the atmosphere in a lesbian home isn't the most conducive—doesn't tend to lead to—well, happiness, mental balance, or whatever."

"Don't you think *we're* balanced?"

"Look, Ali, I love both of you just as you are, but you do seem slightly changed to me since you left, and I don't think it's just your age or whatever."

"But before that, were we balanced then?"

Daddy cleared his throat. "Well, yes, I think . . . of course, you were seeing me, but I think Cynthia did a good job in most ways. There were a few things, but nothing special."

I leaned against him. He felt very solid and warm and comforting. "I wish I could just, you know, definitely want to do one thing or another."

He just sighed. "I know it's hard for you."

"I'm just afraid Mom will mind."

"Ali, listen, if someone kills a man and then another person attempts to put him in jail, do you say, 'But I'm afraid he'll mind'?"

"But Mom didn't *kill* anyone."

"I'm drawing an analogy, darling, just to make it

clearer to you. Look, life involves a lot of decisions that in some way or another affect other people. You have to get used to that."

"If I decide I want to go back, can I?"

He was silent a moment. "I don't know."

"What do you mean?" My heart started pounding.

"I mean that I want you to be where you'll be happiest. I think the part of you that wants to go back to New York is like the little girl clinging to her mommy's skirts, not the action of a grown-up, or half-grown person."

"Can I call Mom and talk to her about it?"

"No, absolutely not. I don't want either of you speaking to her or writing to her until this is clarified."

"But what if she calls here?"

"Don't answer the phone. Eileen and I will answer it. If we're not here, just let it ring."

"Can I write to her?"

"I'd rather you didn't for now."

"Why?"

"Because this is a legal action, darling! The waters are muddied enough as it is without having great carryings on over the phone—hysterical women . . ."

"I wouldn't get hysterical."

"Ali, I've *seen* you when you get off the phone with Cynthia. You look wrung out."

"Only that time she was in the accident."

"Honey, look, about some things I simply know more than you do. You have to accept that. I know a lot about divorce and custody cases, even if it's not my direct field.

And then, well, we're very lucky to have Eileen with her psychiatric background. She knows all the damage such a relationship can cause."

I hated the idea of Daddy and Eileen talking about Mom behind her back. "You once said each case had to be considered separately."

"Of course! But that doesn't mean all other cases have no bearing. Just trust me, okay?"

"Okay," I said finally.

He squeezed my shoulder. "Everything'll be fine, sweetie. Really."

I smiled up at him. "I guess I better get dressed for dinner."

"Right." He got up off the bed. For a second he stood there sort of awkwardly. "It's good we can talk like this," he said.

"Yeah." I felt awkward too.

"I love you."

"Me too. I mean—"

He ducked out of the room. "See you at supper."

As I was getting dressed, I heard the phone ring. I thought of how I wasn't supposed to answer it from now on. I know Daddy's a lawyer, so I guess he knows best. But I wished everything wasn't so complicated. I wished I'd never started liking Ethan, and Gretchen was still my friend, and I was going back to New York. I remembered how excited I'd been on the plane coming to California. If someone had asked me then if I would've liked to live there all year round, I'd have said yes in a second. Now I don't feel so sure.

Thirteen

I told Teddy I'd see him that evening. I wasn't really in the mood, but I didn't feel like canceling it, because I'd canceled our last date. Luckily, we went to a movie, so I didn't have to talk much except about casual things. But on the way back, I began feeling awkward.

"Ali?" Teddy took my hand.

"Umm?"

"Listen, there's something I guess I should tell you."

"What is it?"

"Well, it's about Emily."

"What about her?"

"Well, the thing is, I've been seeing her a little bit."

"You told me that already!"

"No, I mean since you've come out here. It was just—well, you seemed so different, Ali, like you weren't even interested in seeing me that much."

"It wasn't so much that," I said lamely.

"Emily really likes me," Teddy said. And I think since you're going back anyway, well, maybe we should just kind of phase things out with us."

Even though I'd been planning to say more or less the

same thing to Teddy, I felt miffed that he said it first. I wondered what he'd do with his scrapbook, if he'd keep it for some other girl like Emily or what. "Actually, I may be staying here," I said.

"How come? For good, you mean?"

"Maybe. My father's looking into it."

"I thought kids always had to stay with their mother."

"Not necessarily. Anyway, it's not definite yet."

"Do you want to stay?"

"Well, I—I still don't know. It's hard to explain."

"It might be different if you were staying," Teddy said, looking torn.

I couldn't help teasing him. "But you still like Emily and she likes you."

"True," Teddy said, as though savoring that fact.

"I think she's liked you for a long time, actually," I said.

"That's what *she* says," Teddy agreed.

"That's why she was always so awful to me."

"No, you're wrong there, Ali. Emily really *likes* you. It's just she always thought you were funny with her."

I looked up at him. "Will *we* still be friendly?"

"Sure, I want to, don't you?"

I nodded.

"Don't worry, Ali. You'll find someone too, I bet, really soon."

"Oh, I'm not worried," I said. I smiled.

"Elvis likes you. I bet now that he and Sheila—"

"Teddy!"

"Well, you said you might be staying."

"I've never liked Elvis. How can you even *say* that?"

"Okay. I just thought it might be fun—you and him going out with me and Emily."

"Wow!" I said.

"You aren't jealous, are you?" Teddy said, almost hopefully, peering around at me.

"No," I said. That made me think of Gretchen and I felt bad again.

Almost as though he knew what I was thinking, Teddy said, "I bet Gretchen will be glad if you stay."

"Umm," I said. I didn't exactly feel like telling Teddy what had happened with Gretchen and me.

"I guess she'll be glad we broke up."

"No," I said slowly. "I don't think so."

"She never liked me very much."

"Well. . . ."

"Anyhow, she can have you all to herself now," Teddy said.

I didn't like the way that sounded. "That's not what she wants!"

"It sure seems like it."

"It isn't!"

Teddy said, "Listen, I'm not sorry we liked each other, are you?"

"Uh uh."

"I guess we *were* sort of young to have been thinking of getting married and all that."

"You were the one who did that mostly," I said, "with your scrapbook and all."

"I still have it," he said wistfully.

"Teddy, you're so funny, thinking that far ahead. I don't even know what's going to happen two *weeks* from now!"

"I don't see what's wrong with planning for the future," he said stiffly.

"No, I didn't say it's wrong."

"That doesn't mean it'll turn out *exactly* the way you plan, but you should still know a little bit—"

"Sure," I said quickly.

When we came back to the house, I asked if he wanted to come in again for a little while.

"I guess I better not," Teddy said smiling in an embarrassed way. "No point in starting everything up again."

"I didn't mean—"

"No, it's just. . . ." He looked embarrassed. "I wouldn't want Emily to think, *you* know . . ."

"I understand." I looked up and kissed him. "Don't worry about it."

He looked pleased. "I'll be seeing you, Ali."

After Teddy left I went into the kitchen to fix a snack for myself. I didn't feel so terrible now that I'd gotten over the idea that he'd wanted to say it first. I'm glad we never made love though. It would have been nice making love with Teddy in a lot of ways. He's so warm and, well, cuddly, like a teddy bear. But still, I think the first time it should be with someone you really love. Even if it's not the person you end up marrying, I think you should feel like you really love that person and they love you.

Eileen looked in. She had her bathrobe on, a red one with her initials monogrammed on the collar in gold: *E A R*. It looked funny. I wondered what the *A* was for.

"Is the *A* for your middle name?" I asked.

"Oh." She looked down, as though she'd forgotten it was there. "No, that's my maiden name, *Aiken*." She sat down. "You're back early."

"Well, we just saw one movie. We didn't feel like seeing the double feature."

"Didn't Teddy want to come in for something to eat?"

I hate the way Eileen does that, questioning you about everything. I shook my head.

"He seems very fond of you," she said, smiling.

"Yeah, pretty much," I said, "but, well, we're not as close as we once were."

"You're so young, awfully young to be close to someone in that way."

"Well, I don't think it's a matter of age so much," I said. I didn't want to tell her about Ethan.

"There's no point in rushing things is all I meant." Eileen opened the refrigerator door. She took out a can of carrot juice, opened it, and poured it into a glass. I've tried it since we came here. It's not as bad as you'd expect, but still not so great. "So . . . Ali," she said.

"What?" I said.

"I feel very—well, maybe touched isn't the right word, but I'm so happy you and Martin are thinking of staying here."

I swallowed. "Yeah, well, I haven't actually decided."

"I think it's going to be such a good thing for both of

you. Harold has always been so eager for it, but he never realized, he never understood the whole picture until now."

Just then the phone rang. I got up and started walking to it, but Eileen intercepted it quietly but swiftly. "No, I'm sorry, she's not in now," she said. "Can I take a message? Yes, I'll tell her."

"Who was that?" I said after she'd hung up.

"Your mother's friend."

"Has she been calling a lot?"

"A few times."

"I don't see why I can't speak to her," I said, frowning.

"Well, in a legal matter like this, we have to stand by Harold's decision. He knows so much more about this than we do."

"Is he scared I'll decide to go back with Mom? Is that it?"

"He wants what's best for you, Ali, and he's just afraid that—well, sometimes you *can* be rather impulsive, you know."

"But what if Mom gets worried and thinks something is wrong."

"Obviously, something *is* wrong," Eileen said. "That's what we're trying to bring across. And I'm sure once she gets Harold's letter, everything will be clear."

"What letter?"

"He's writing to Cynthia, didn't he tell you? He just felt a simple, clear letter laying everything out would be best for everyone."

I felt bad thinking of Mom getting the letter. "What's he going to say?"

"Just the facts—about you and Martin and how we feel about what's happening."

"Why can't *I* write too?"

"You can—later on, of course."

"But why not *now?*"

"Ali, you have to realize that Harold knows infinitely more about these things than either you or I will ever know."

"Still—"

"You see, this is precisely what's been lacking so far, for both of you—a sense of having parents in the *real* sense, who put your welfare before any personal desires."

"I think Mom was doing a pretty good job," I said.

"Of course she was," Eileen said carefully, "to the extent that she *could*, living that kind of life."

"*What* kind?"

"Well, her whole relationship with this other woman —she *had* to have known how injurious that would be to two children. She can't *not* have known that!"

"But Daddy doesn't even know that's true!"

"He knows," Eileen said with a kind of smile.

"All he knows is what I told him."

"Ali, remember, he's known Cynthia a lot longer than you have. He has a whole background of facts to go by. Aren't you willing to trust him?"

"I guess," I said. Every time I tried to talk about it to

anyone, I just got more mixed up. "I wish Mom had never moved to New York!"

"That's how you feel now," Eileen said, "but a few months from now, when all the dust has settled, I think you'll be glad. It's giving us all a chance to clarify things."

"What if Mom says she'll move back here?"

"How can she? Her job is in New York."

"Maybe she'd give up her job."

"Anyway, the job isn't the point, Ali. It doesn't matter where she *lives*."

"It does to me."

"I know, but you aren't the best judge right now about what would be best for you. Mere geographic location isn't what's at stake here."

Talking to Eileen tired me out. I couldn't seem to make her understand what I felt, no matter how much I tried. I sat there, rubbing my finger along the tabletop.

"You look tired," Eileen said softly.

"I am sort of." I got up and stretched. "Well, I'll see you in the morning," I said.

"Sleep well, dear."

In bed I kept thinking of Mom and Peggy. I wonder if they're home or still in that place in Vermont. I wonder what the lodge is like. I kept wondering what would have happened if I'd decided to join Mom there like she'd suggested on the phone. Maybe that would've been better.

Fourteen

In the morning Martin was having breakfast when I came into the kitchen. In some ways, I wish Martin was my sister. If he was, I could ask him more about the thing with Tess. I wonder if they go to bed and make love and fall asleep from, say, twelve to six, and then he comes home. Or do they make love all night, so he doesn't even sleep at all? He never *looks* especially tired, though sometimes he yawns.

"Aren't Tess's parents coming home soon?" I asked.

"Friday," Martin said gloomily.

"Well, at least you had three weeks," I pointed out.

"Yeah." He looked morose. "Actually, we may get married."

"What?"

He laughed. "What's wrong?"

"I thought you weren't getting married till you were thirty!"

"Yeah, well, but I meant married in that sense of having kids and settling down and stuff like that. We'd just be getting married so we could be together."

"Oh." I thought a minute. "But won't her parents have a fit?"

"Probably. Look, it isn't definite or anything. It's just something we've talked about."

"So, you must really be in love, huh?"

Martin grinned sheepishly.

"Is it because of sex?" I asked.

He looked startled. "Is what because of sex?"

I blushed. "I mean, is it because her parents were away and you—"

"Well, sex changes things," he said, as though that were a matter of course.

"How?"

"*How?*" He looked amused. "What do you mean *how?*"

"I just mean how? *How* does it change things?"

I could see that Martin was torn between joking around and answering me straight. Finally he said slowly, "Well, it deepens whatever you already feel."

"Does it always?"

"Why? Are you and Ethan—"

"Martin, come *on!*"

"I just thought there might be a reason for this sudden curiosity."

"Look, I'm only fifteen."

"So?"

"Well, don't you think that's a little young?"

"Not especially. I mean, when you're ready, you're ready. Some people are ready at twelve."

"You mean, like in primitive tribes and stuff like that?"

He laughed. "No, right here, in Berkeley."

"At *twelve?*"

"Sure."

"Ethan hasn't had that much experience with girls."

"Yeah, he doesn't look the type that would've."

"What do you mean?" I said huffily, even though I knew.

"I'm not being critical. He just seems kind of a loner."

I looked at Martin for a minute. "I like him a lot."

Martin smiled at me in an affectionate way. "Good."

Sometimes Martin can be unexpectedly nice.

After breakfast I tried calling Gretchen. Ethan answered. "Hi, Ali," he said in a low voice.

"Is Gretchen still mad?" I asked.

"She's in the living room," he said, which I knew meant he couldn't talk freely.

"I feel so *bad*, Ethan," I said. "Do you think I should come over? Could I speak to her?"

"Maybe not now," he said.

"Will you come over here then?"

"Is after lunch all right?"

"Sure. Can you tell her I called anyway."

"Okay."

One minute later the phone rang. I picked it up. It was Mom. "Is that you, Ali?"

I didn't say anything. I felt so scared after everything Daddy had said. I didn't want to do anything wrong.

"Ali? Are you there? Listen, tell me. I've just been frantic trying to get hold of you. What's going on?"

"I'm—I'm not supposed to talk to you," I stammered.

"Why, darling? What's been going *on?* Please tell me, I beg you! I don't understand it."

"I just can't, I—" I hung up and burst into tears.

About one minute later the phone started to ring again. I ran outside and put my hands over my ears, not wanting to hear the ringing. It sounded like someone screaming. I felt terrible! Mom sounded so worried. Why is it wrong to talk to her?

I kept thinking I could still hear the phone ringing, but after about fifteen minutes I went back to the house and it had stopped. I took the receiver off the hook and put it in a drawer. Of course, it might be Daddy or Eileen. But I wasn't supposed to answer it and I was the only person home.

Peggy has a phone in her bathroom back in New York. She once told me she liked to talk to people while she is in the bath. Once I came in and she was there in the tub, talking to this friend. She even has magazines you can read while you're in there.

Even though I was glad the phone wasn't ringing anymore, the quietness of everything made me nervous. I kept wondering what Mom had done after she hung up, whether she was still trying to reach me. I began thinking of this book I had liked when I was young, about a group of girls who were all orphans. They lived together in this big house near the sea. I don't know if it was realistic or not, but none of them ever seemed to wish they had parents or even think of having them. They had so much fun, millions of adventures. I used to wish even then that I could be an orphan too.

When Mom and Daddy first got divorced, I had this thing of not wanting to go to school, which I don't think had anything to do with that but more with this teacher I had that year—I didn't like her at all! But Mom thought it was because of the divorce, and I had to go talk to this psychologist. He kept trying to get me to say I thought Mom and Daddy really hated each other, but I *didn't*. I didn't think they did. I never heard them yelling at each other the way Gretchen hears her mother and Roger. That's why I was kind of surprised when they decided to get divorced. Of course, I was only eight, so maybe I just hadn't noticed so much.

Now I can't help wondering if they really do hate each other or if Daddy just wants us with him because he thinks he'll be a better parent. I fixed a sandwich, but after about two mouthfuls I couldn't eat any more. I went outside again to wait for Ethan.

When I saw him coming down the road, I jumped up. "So, how are things?" he said in his quiet voice. All of a sudden I began to cry. I hadn't even known I was going to, but once I started I couldn't stop. Ethan patted me on the shoulder, hugging me. "It's okay, Ali. Don't cry. It'll be okay."

I couldn't even speak for a long time. "Why does everyone *hate* each other so much?" I whispered.

"Gretchen doesn't *hate* you," he said, stroking my hair. "She's just kind of—confused, I guess."

"She *does* hate me," I said. "I know it."

"No, it isn't that," he said. "It's just that since our parents get along the way they do, she's always looked to me to have someone to talk to, like I was a parent to her. Maybe that was my fault, encouraging her."

"What else could you have done?"

"I don't know. But I feel like I'm as much to blame as you are in this."

"You're not, Ethan, really. It was *my* fault. Did you know she wasn't even asleep when we carried her in?"

"She told me."

"It was like she was spying on us!"

"Well . . ." Ethan looked perplexed. He sighed.

"I wish she had really been asleep."

"That wouldn't have solved anything. She'd have found out eventually."

"Not if I'd gone back to New York."

"If we wrote each other, she would have."

"What should I *do* though? Should I write her a letter? Would she even read it?"

"Sure she would. She might not answer it though."

I sat down on the stone fence. Ethan sat next to me. I told him about Mom and the phone ringing.

"Why didn't you answer it when she called back?" he said puzzled.

"Daddy said not to! He'd have been furious if I did."

"Are you that scared of him?"

"It's not that, Ethan. I mean Daddy's a *lawyer*. He really knows about all of this, and I don't know *anything*."

"He just wants to keep you."

"But that's because he loves me, so it can't be bad, can it? I mean he really thinks it would be better for us."

"I never liked your father that much," Ethan said.

"You don't even *know* him!"

"I've met him a couple of times."

"You can't judge from that! Anyway, even if you *don't* like him, that doesn't mean he isn't a good lawyer and doesn't know about all this stuff."

"Ali, you're so—"

"What?"

"I don't know . . . malleable. It's like the thing with Teddy. You let other people push you around. You let *their* feelings determine what *you* do."

"But I want to do the right thing," I said, afraid he was right.

"So do what really feels best to *you*. Don't go around taking a straw poll of everyone you know. Who do *you* really want to live with?"

"You mean, if it weren't for you and Gretchen?"

"Yes."

I sighed. "I don't know. Mom, I guess, but I feel mixed up. I just—" I bit my lip. I was afraid I might start crying again.

"Don't, Ali." He still had his arm around me. I leaned back against him and closed my eyes. He felt warm and solid. "What do you really want?" Ethan said softly.

"To have no one mad at me."

He smiled. "I don't think anyone's mad at you. Everyone just wants different things from you, and you can't please them all."

"Why not?"

"It just doesn't work that way."

"I don't see why." I sighed. "I know it's childish but partly I wish everything would just happen, that someone would decide *for* me so it wouldn't be my responsibility so much."

Just sitting there next to Ethan made me feel better. When I was with him, the whole thing of Mom and Daddy and all the fighting seemed far away. I forgot about the phone and not having to answer it, and how scared Mom had sounded, and all of Daddy's probing and questioning.

While we were sitting there, Martin came along. "Hi, Ali, Ethan," he said as he passed us. He was dressed in tennis shorts and a shirt. He walked right into the house, but a moment later he came out again. "Hey, Ali," he said, "you left the phone off the hook."

"Oh," I said, "well . . ."

"I put it back on."

After Martin had left, I said, "It's hard for me to talk to him about things."

"Yeah, I know what you mean."

"He's always so—cool in a way, like nothing ever bothers him."

"That's just a cover-up probably."

"I don't know. Maybe with Tess he's different, but with me he usually acts like I'm some little twerp, and it isn't worth his time to even talk to me seriously about anything. I guess that's why I like the way you treat Gretchen so much. You never talk down to her just because you're older."

"Well, that's partly because Gretchen is so—well, she doesn't seem to know how to take care of herself."

"Do *I* seem to?" I said.

"In a way. Maybe not about this, but in general more than her. She looks up to you for being able to handle all that."

"All what?"

"Just, you know, being relaxed with boys and that kind of thing. You know how she is."

I nodded. "Sometimes I wish I'd never started liking you," I said quietly.

"You can stop," he suggested with a smile.

"No, I can't! That's the trouble."

Ethan kept stroking the back of my hand, going up along my fingers and nails and then down again. It gave me sort of a tingling feeling, even though it was just my hand. Finally he said, "I guess I should go back, Ali."

"Okay," I said. But I felt hurt by the way he said it, as though he'd been staying just to please me, because I was so upset.

"What's the matter?" he said. He was standing right in front of me.

"You act like you're doing me a big favor, just by coming over."

"Ali, come on, you *know* that's not true. I thought we had such a nice talk."

"It's just . . ." I looked right at him. "I thought we were going to spend more time together."

"Do you want me to stay? I wasn't sure."

I added. "Why don't we go to my room? It's more private, sort of."

We went inside the house. I locked the door to my room. Ethan stood there, staring at me. He looked as if he couldn't decide what to do. Then he came over, put his arms around me, and kissed me. I kissed him back as hard as I could.

"I'm sorry," I whispered.

"About what?"

"I feel—I don't know." I felt like I wanted to lie in bed with him, but I couldn't say it.

"Do you want to lie down?" he asked after a minute.

I didn't know if he meant did I want to rest just by myself or what. I took off my sandals and lay down. He was still standing there.

"Do you want me to stay?"

I nodded.

We lay there, side by side. It was awkward, it being afternoon and Martin being in the house. But once we started kissing, it was good. I didn't think of anything but that.

"Look, Ali, I don't know if—"

"What?"

He looked embarrassed. "Well, if we keep doing this, we'll probably end up. . . ."

"So?" I felt really hurt.

"It's just that you have this problem with your mother. I don't want to take advantage of—"

"You're not" I said.

He pulled me close to him. "I want you, don't you see? It's difficult. I feel badly about Gretchen too. This happened so fast."

"I know," I said softly, feeling better.

"I think about you all the time." He smiled. "I feel

like I don't think about anything else, but maybe it'll be better for both of us if we try to go slowly."

"But what if I go back to New York?"

"I'm applying to Columbia. I might have to go there for an interview."

"Really? You never mentioned that."

"It's not just for you," he said. "The going slowly part, I mean. It'd be hypocritical if I said that. It's for me too. I don't—well—form attachments to people lightly."

"I know," I said, kissing his collarbone.

"I don't want either of us to feel we acted on the impulse of a moment and then had second thoughts."

"It's *not* the impulse of a moment!" I said indignantly. "We've known each other five *years!*"

"You know what I mean."

"Ethan, did you ever, like—"

"What?"

"Well, think about me that way before this summer? You know, as a girlfriend?"

He smiled. "I fantasized about it. I never thought of it as a possible thing."

"Why not?"

"Well, you're so pretty and you always seemed to have boyfriends. I didn't think I was your type."

"I didn't think I was *your* type. I thought you thought I was a bubble-brain. I'd go babbling on and you'd just kind of look at me, like you were thinking, 'Can't she say *anything* smart?' "

"I was probably too scared to open my mouth."

"But even when I wore my new bikini, you didn't say anything!"

"I was stunned."

"Did you notice it?"

"Sure."

"Did you like it?"

"I liked you *in* it. You looked like a daydream someone decided to bring to life."

I hugged him. "I love you so much!"

"I love you too, Ali."

"I think you're right, we *should* wait. It's just sometimes—"

"I know. It'll happen, and when it does, it'll be terrific."

"Do you really think so?"

"Yes."

We looked at each other and laughed, nervously.

"Everything will work out. Don't worry."

"Okay," I said.

"Call me later, all right?"

I nodded. Just as he left, the phone started ringing again. I went in to take a shower. I knew I wouldn't hear anything with the water running.

Fifteen

That night Daddy, Eileen, and I were having supper when we heard the sound of a car pulling up outside. Martin was eating out with Tess. We were just about up to dessert.

"Did Martin take the car?" Eileen asked.

"I don't think so," Daddy said. "Did you give him the keys?"

"I can't remember. There's that extra pair—"

Suddenly the kitchen door swung open and Mom walked in. She was on crutches and one of her legs was in a cast, but otherwise she looked the same. "Mom!" I cried out.

"Hi, Ali," she said in a very quiet voice. "Where's Martin?"

"He's, um, out with Tess," I stammered.

"Cynthia, look. I don't think this makes sense. I thought you had received my letter," Daddy said.

"I think Ali and I have a lot to talk about," Mom said.

"I'm afraid I can't allow that," Daddy said.

"I'm afraid I don't give a damn *what* you'll allow," Mom said. She leaned her crutches against the wall. "Could I have some coffee?" she asked.

I jumped up and poured her some. "Do you want some dessert?" I said.

"I ate on the plane, thanks, sweetie," Mom said. When she talked to me, her voice was completely different than when she talked to Daddy.

Eileen was staring at Mom as though she couldn't think of a thing to say. "How did you get here?" she asked.

"I took a cab from the airport," Mom said.

We all sat in silence for a minute. Mom sipped her coffee. "Please go on with your meal," she said ironically. "I don't want to disturb anything."

"Cynthia, this is extraordinarily irresponsible," Daddy said.

"Well, there've been a lot of extraordinary things going on," Mom said calmly. "I don't think this is the most flagrant by any means."

"This all should be handled by lawyers," Daddy said. "Ali, would you go to your room, please?"

I looked pleadingly at Mom. "Should I?" I said.

"Of course not," Mom said. "It's you I want to talk to, Ali."

"That's absolutely out of the question," Daddy said. "Ali, please."

"But I want to—"

"Ali, Harold knows what he's talking about," Eileen said. "There are legal complications in all of this."

"Will you both leave her alone!" Mom said. "This minute."

"But I said that—"

"Look, let's get one thing straight," Mom said. "I've come here to talk to Ali alone, without anyone listening in, and I'm not leaving until I do."

"Then we may have to simply force you to leave, Cynthia," Daddy said, "which I shouldn't have to say would be a rather ugly scene."

"Force me?" Mom said dryly. "What? Throw me out with my crutches?"

"If you thought for one *second* about Alison's welfare . . ." Daddy began.

"Harold, I don't even want to talk about this with you," Mom said, "till I've talked to Ali, okay? So save your breath."

I began feeling like I had to throw up. I tried pinching the palm of my hand, saying to myself, *Please don't let me throw up, please don't let me throw up.* "I—uh—feel sort of funny," I said finally. I ran into the bathroom just in time. My whole meal practically came back up. When I was finished, I had a sour taste in my mouth but I felt a little better.

Daddy, Eileen, and Mom came rushing in after me. "You see!" Daddy said. "*Look* at her! Is this what you want?"

"No, it isn't," Mom said. "I didn't start this whole thing. I hate it. I hate what you're doing to her, using her this way. God, it makes me *sick*. Don't you give a damn about anyone but yourself?"

"Myself!" Daddy said. "I certainly do. I care about my children and the way they're being brought up. I care about that very much."

"It doesn't look like it, does it?" Mom said. She put her hand on my shoulder. "How do you feel, sweetie?"

"Better," I whispered, hanging onto the sink.

"Have a little water," Mom said. "Rinse your mouth out."

I did that while the three of them stood watching me.

"I think we ought to leave this whole thing up to Alison," Eileen said.

"Good idea," Mom said.

"Would you like to talk to your mother?" Eileen asked.

"I simply won't allow it," Daddy said before I could speak.

"Harold, I think—" Eileen began.

"Eileen, please!" Daddy said. "Let *me* handle this."

"I was trying to be helpful," Eileen said, looking hurt.

"Ali is in much too confused a state right now to go through an ordeal like this," Daddy said.

"It's no wonder she is!" Mom said.

"You *see* the state she's in. What are you trying to do to her?" he said to Mom.

"Harold!" Mom said.

"She's my daughter too," Daddy said.

"Then why in God's name are you putting her through a thing like this?"

"I want what will be best for her. That's all. I want her to live in a home where . . . to know what it's like to live in a normal, happy home."

"If this is a normal, happy home, God save us all," Mom said.

"It was, until you walked in the door. All has been *fine* until now."

"That's a lie," Mom said.

"You haven't even *been* here! You don't know how relieved she was when I suggested the possibility of her living here. You should have seen her face."

"I didn't have to," Mom said. "I spoke to her on the phone. Her voice was shaking. She sounded terrified."

"Because she was scared you'd come and get her."

"Because she was bewildered by all these orders, *that's* why," Mom said.

It was odd in a way having them talk about me as though I wasn't even there.

"Why are you so frightened of us having a talk, Harold?" Mom said in a softer voice. "What exactly are you afraid of?"

"You're going to make her feel guilty and upset about staying here."

"I swear I won't."

"Why can't you speak in front of us?"

"Because what I have to say is private." Mom looked at me. "Do you want to talk to me, Ali? If you don't, I'll go home."

I was terrified Daddy would get mad at me, but I said, "Yes, I'd like to."

"This is precisely what I was afraid of," Daddy said.

"I don't think a *talk* would hurt anything," Eileen said.

"Eileen, what did I just say? I can handle this myself!" Daddy looked furious.

"Are we going to the Goldmans' or not?" Eileen said. "Can I ask that?"

"Oh Lord, tonight?"

"Yes, they said eight thirty and it's almost nine."

Daddy sighed. "I don't know," he said. He looked at Mom. "Will you give me your word that Alison will be here when I get back?"

"I can," Mom said. "In fact, I'll be here too. I'm planning to stay the night."

"You can sleep in my room," I said. "I have a fold-up bed."

Daddy said, "Okay, look, obviously I have no choice in the matter, but I want to warn you Cynthia, if Alison is *not* here—"

"I gave you my word of honor," Mom said, deadpan.

"I'll be here, Daddy," I said. I was still afraid he was mad at me. "I promise."

Daddy looked uncertain, as though he still wasn't sure.

"Darling, we should set off," Eileen said. She was getting her coat from the closet.

"We'll be back early," Daddy said.

"Well I don't think we can leave *too* early," Eileen said. "If we don't get there till past nine."

"Eileen, please! I'll just drop you off and come back. You can stay as long as you want."

"But should I explain what happened?"

"Of course not! To the Goldmans?"

"Sylvia is a lawyer."

"I don't care *what* she is. I will not have one word of this spoken about."

"Okay, I *heard* you!"

Daddy turned around to look at me again. "You're sure you'll be okay, Ali? How are you feeling?"

I still had that sour, throw-up feeling in my throat, but I just said, "I'm okay, Daddy. Really."

After Daddy and Eileen left, there was this sort of awkward silence. "Would you like to see my room?" I said to Mom, feeling shy with her.

"Yes, I'd love to," she said softly.

We went into the room. Mom smiled. "It's just the way you described it."

"I've gotten used to it," I said. "I don't mind it so much any more."

"I used to want a four-poster bed when I was little," Mom said.

"Eileen did too," I said.

Mom just stood there, looking at me. Then she hugged me really close. "Oh, sweetie, I'm so sorry for this horrible, horrible mess. I can't tell you. When I spoke to you on the phone and you hung up, it was. . . ." She broke off.

"I wanted to speak to you," I said. "I really did. It was just that Daddy said—"

"I know, darling."

"I thought he must know what he was doing," I said, "since he's a lawyer and everything."

Mom sat down on the bed. "Tell me, though, how *do*

you really feel, Ali? Do you want to stay here or do you want to go back with me?"

"I don't *know*," I said desperately. "I'm so mixed up now!"

Mom sighed. "I can't imagine how this whole thing got started. You've been out here such a short time! And I've always been so revoltingly scrupulous with you and Martin, not saying anything about Harold behind his back. It just puzzles me that he would want to do this."

"He said it was because of us. He said it was because he loved us."

"Sure," Mom said. "I guess that's as good an excuse as any."

"It's *my* fault, really," I said slowly.

"What is?"

"That Daddy got the idea of keeping us."

"Did you tell him you wanted to stay?"

"No, but . . . it was just, well, the first night we were here I was telling him about that time Peggy and you stayed in her apartment, and Daddy kept questioning us about it. It seemed like it somehow planted this idea in his head."

"What idea?"

I swallowed. "Well, just about you and Peggy." I felt nervous so I rushed on. "He was afraid, like, that a robber might have come. You know, he thinks in New York it's so dangerous and everything."

"So it wasn't basically the thing about my staying with Peggy that bothered him?"

"I don't know."

"What do you think, Ali? Tell me."

"About what?"

"About me and Peggy."

I tried to laugh. "It's probably not even true, what he said."

"What did he say?"

"Well, he just kept saying maybe you and Peggy, you know, loved each other, weren't just friends."

"Did that upset you?"

I shrugged.

"Do you think it's true, sweetheart?"

"Well, I think if it was, you'd have told us, because you're always saying we should be open about what we feel."

"That's true," Mom said.

"I don't think there's anything wrong with it," I said quickly. "I mean, I'm not prejudiced or anything."

"Darn it. This is so hard for me, Ali. I better take a big breath and just say it. . . . It's true."

I didn't know what to say. "Yeah, well, I guess a lot of people are that way," I said. That sounded stupid and awful, but I didn't know what would sound better.

"I feel terrible that I didn't tell you, Ali. I should have. That was really wrong."

"Why didn't you then?"

Mom looked pensive. "I was just afraid. I don't know. I felt you'd both been through so much with the divorce. I thought it would be an extra burden for you to carry around. But I was wrong. I see that now."

"That's okay," I said. "Now I know."

Mom smiled. "Now you know," she said. "*Does* it make you uncomfortable?"

"I don't know. I don't think so."

"It would be natural if it did. Don't feel ashamed if you feel funny about it."

"I guess I *was* sort of hoping it wouldn't be true," I admitted.

"It *would* make things easier," Mom said. "There's no doubt about that." She drew her finger along the edge of the bed. "Ali, listen, I do love Peggy and we've even been thinking that next year we'd get a bigger apartment and share it, one big enough for all four of us. But I don't want you to come unless you feel—I don't know how to put this, but unless it would be what *you* want, all by yourself, not because Harold or Eileen or I was pressuring you."

"How come we couldn't stay in the brownstone?" I asked.

"We just thought for the rent we're both spending we could get a better deal that way. We don't need two kitchens, for instance."

"Would it be far away from where we are now?"

"No, not necessarily. Don't you like the neighborhood? I do."

"Yeah, I like it too," I said.

"You'd have your own bedroom, the same as now. Martin could have the other one, and Peggy and I could use, well, if there's a separate dining room we could use that."

"Mom?"

"Yes?"

"If Martin does decide to stay out here, it'll be because of Tess."

Mom smiled. "I know, honey. But it isn't *just* that."

"He says home is where you set down your things. I think that's what he said."

"Martin covers up an awful lot about how he feels. He's not like you. One look at you and I know what you're feeling; but Martin, well, maybe it's helped me through some of the tough spots. He hasn't crumpled under."

"He's like Daddy, sort of," I said.

"Well, in a sense, but not really," Mom said. "I don't think Martin uses people the same way Harold does. There isn't so much manipulation involved."

"How come you got married though," I said. "If . . ."

"If I prefer women to men?"

"Sort of."

"I didn't know then. It was just something I'd had thoughts about. And I loved Harold. It wasn't a marriage of convenience or anything. I thought we'd make it together. Maybe I was naïve. And things were so different then, so much more closed off. If you felt the way I did, you felt guilty. *I* did, anyhow. I fought it off for years, thinking I could get over it that way."

"Was Peggy the same way? About fighting it off?"

"Not so much. Of course in New York it's freer anyway. She's lived with other women since she got out of college."

"How come she didn't stay with any of them?"

"It's the same as with marriage. You don't know how it'll work out. You just hope."

I frowned. "I wish you *could* know how it would turn out," I said suddenly.

"I know, honey. We all wish that."

"Mom," I said. "Really, the reason I wanted to stay here was because of Ethan and Gretchen."

"What do you mean?"

"Well, I started liking Ethan this summer and Gretchen is so angry, like she really *hates* me. When I call her house, she won't even *speak* to me!"

"That sounds pretty childish," Mom said.

"She feels like I sort of betrayed her and came between her and Ethan."

"Strange."

"Still, that's just the way she feels. If I'd known she felt that way so much, I never would have started liking him."

Mom frowned. "You've had quite a summer, haven't you?"

"Do you think Gretchen will keep on being angry with me?"

"I don't know, honey. These things are tricky."

"I don't see why I can't like both of them, do you?"

"Of course not, but Gretchen's always taken your friendship too seriously. Remember how mad she used to get when you invited other girls over to the house?"

I'd forgotten all about that. "Ethan is so nice!" I said.

"He *is* a nice boy," Mom said. "I always thought that."

"I didn't mean to do anything to hurt her feelings—I really didn't."

"Of course you didn't sweetie. No one's accusing you. Anyway, if you're away from the problem for a while, it will sort itself out. That often happens."

"I guess I *do* want to go back," I said.

"Don't say it unless you really want to," Mom said. "Sleep on it."

I couldn't help laughing. "That's such a funny expression."

"No, I mean it, Ali. Don't do it because you think I'll be mad at you if you stay. Don't let that enter into it."

"But would you be?"

"I'd like to see you where you'll be happy."

"I don't really like Eileen," I said. I felt good being able to tell someone that. "She's so sort of, I don't know, I can't *describe* it—sort of prying."

"She's probably awkward with you."

"But how come? She's known us five years!"

"She's probably trying to please Harold too. He wants you to like her; it means a lot to him."

"But he used to say we weren't being fair or giving her a chance. I tried to, like you said, be friendly."

"That's fine. How else can you act? You can't force love, or even liking, for that matter."

I sighed. "I wish I could be two people," I said, "so I could do both things and no one would be mad at me."

"Honey, forget about the mad thing."

"I can't!"

"Yes, you can. You're pretty big now."

I looked up. "Should we get out the folding bed?" I asked. "It's in the closet."

I crawled in the closet and got the bed from the back. We put sheets and a blanket on it.

"How's the weather been out here?" Mom asked. "It's been ferociously hot in New York."

"It's a drought," I said. "Mom, take that end . . . no, the other one. Okay, you do the bottom and I'll do the top."

Mom was kind of hobbling around on her crutches. She seemed pretty lively.

"Does it hurt you to walk?" I asked.

"No, not to speak of. We were so lucky with that accident!"

"Lucky?"

"Well, we were teetering right on the edge of a ravine. We could easily have fallen over."

"I'm glad you didn't," I said.

Mom laughed. "Me too."

I got into my pajamas. Mom hadn't brought any, so I lent her a pair of mine. They fit pretty well, although they were a little tight around the waist.

"Will you mind if Martin stays here?" I asked.

"Well, I always thought it was too bad in a way, taking him away from his sports."

I didn't know whether to tell Mom about Martin and Tess and how they might get married. I decided not to. "But would you rather he came back?"

"Of course! Honey, listen, I'm trying to be . . . well,

179

objective, if I can, but certainly I want him to come back. Don't you?"

"Yeah, I guess."

"Just wait. When you're both grown-ups, you'll be perfectly friendly and forget all the wrangling. That's how it was with my brother and me."

When the lights were off, I whispered, "Mom?"

"Yes?"

"The thing I'm afraid of is Daddy won't *let* me come with you."

"He'll let you."

"But he kept talking about taking it to court and everything."

"He won't take it to court," Mom said. "Don't worry about it, sweetheart."

"He might. He's a lawyer and he knows all sorts of things."

"We can get our own lawyer. Don't worry Ali. The only thing that counts if for you to make up your own mind."

"Sure."

As I was lying there, I thought about Mom and Peggy. Maybe I really knew all along, deep down, but just didn't want to think about it, because I didn't really feel as surprised or shocked as I would have expected. It did seem strange in a way, but not *that* strange. Maybe it was because Mom is such a regular sort of person, not that far-out or weird in any way, so it seems like anything she would do would be okay. I wonder if Mom loves Peggy more than she used to love Daddy when she loved him.

Mom reached over and patted my head. "I've had one shampoo bottle all summer," she said. "Can you believe it?"

What she meant was at home I'm always washing my hair, practically every day, and I always forget to write shampoo on the list. We lay in the dark a little while without talking. It was almost like we were having a sleep-over party. "Sweet dreams, Mom," I said finally.

"You too, Ali."

I thought I'd fall right asleep, but I didn't. I lay there thinking about everything until I heard the door open. It was Daddy looking in my room. I closed my eyes and pretended to be asleep. After he'd left I sat up in bed. I guess he'd just dropped Eileen off and come home. He must've really been afraid Mom and I would take off or something.

Suddenly Mom said in this sleepy voice. "Go to sleep, Ali. Don't worry about it."

"Mom, are you awake?"

"Not really. Sleep tight, sweetheart."

Sixteen

When I woke up in the morning, Mom's bed was empty.
I felt scared. I wondered if Daddy had made her go back
to New York or something.

I went out into the front hall. No one seemed to be
around. "Mom?" I called.

"Ali?" It was Daddy.

"What happened to Mom?"

"She and Martin went for a walk."

"Oh." I looked up at him and then away.

"So, how'd it go?" he said.

"How'd what go?"

"Your talk."

"Okay."

"Don't you want to tell me about it?"

I felt embarrassed. "Sure." We went into the living
room and sat down. "I guess I will go back," I said. "I
think that's what I'd rather do."

Daddy just looked at me for a long time, as though
thinking something over. "Did, uh, Cynthia clarify
anything about her relationship with her friend?"

"Daddy, the thing is, I feel like what we talked about is sort of personal. I mean, like, I don't tell Mom things you tell me, if I think you wouldn't want me to."

"Well, I suppose the main thing is whether you feel you can be comfortable with the situation, whatever it is."

"Yeah," I agreed.

"And you think you can?"

I nodded.

We sat staring at each other. Daddy looked pretty grim. "It'll be okay," I said, trying to cheer him up. "Really."

"Well, I thought about it a lot last night," he said, almost as if he was talking to himself. "You've had all these changes, and Eileen feels that maybe another one coming on top of everything else would be bad. She says children that go from one home to another—well, it can be disorienting. And then it's true, I think Cynthia has been, on the whole, concerned with your welfare. I have to give her credit for that."

"Anyway, Martin's staying," I said, "so you'll have him."

He smiled. "Yes, but he's not you. There's only one you."

"Well." I didn't know what to say.

"Ali?"

"Yeah?"

"Promise me one thing. If, when you get back, you find the situation is uncomfortable for you in any way, that you can't handle it, call me. Let me know what's really going on. You can always move back here any time you feel like it, if you change your mind. This doesn't have to be a final decision."

"Okay," I said. I cleared my throat. "Daddy?"

"What?" He looked perplexed.

"You know, Peggy's a really nice person. Maybe if you come to New York some day, you could meet her."

"Yes, well—"

"It's not like what you think." I went over and hugged him; he looked so forlorn. "Things will be okay," I said softly.

"Sure." He smiled in a kind of trying-to-look-on-the-bright-side way. "Well! I guess I'd better set off for the office. Have a good trip back, honey. Call me when you get there."

I wonder if a time will ever come when Daddy'll talk to me in a relaxed way. It's as though my being his daughter puts him in this funny position, and he can't figure out exactly how to act.

Martin and Mom were gone a long time. I went in and started packing. I was all done by the time they got back. Mom looked in the room. I'd folded up her bed and put it back in the closet.

"Oh thanks, Ali. I was going to make it."

"Is Martin staying here with Daddy?" I asked.

Mom nodded. "Yeah, it seems like he and Tess *are* pretty—"

"Are they going to get married?"

"Married?" Mom looked horrified.

I swallowed. "Well, I just—"

"Hon, slow down a little! He's just seventeen."

"Sure."

"I mean, at least kids should make *different* mistakes from their parents."

Just then Martin looked in. "Hey Mom, listen, I've got to go. Take care, okay? Have a good year, Ali." He came over and gave me a hug.

"We'll miss you," Mom said, hugging him too.

"We will?" I said jokingly.

He grinned. "I'll probably miss you too."

"Sure," I said.

"I'll bet you'll miss my typewriter," he said to me.

I blushed. "Hey, that's right. It's still in New York. Can I keep it?"

"Are you kidding? It's almost brand new!"

"I didn't know you liked it so much, Ali," Mom said. "Maybe we can think of something like that for your sixteenth birthday."

"Sweet sixteen," Martin said, smiling at me, "and never been—"

I socked him.

I followed Martin outside. "So, are you getting married or what?" I whispered.

"Married?" He looked almost as surprised as Mom.

"You said—"

"Oh, that. No, that was just when we figured we wouldn't be able to be together."

I looked up at him. "Marty? Did Tess's parents ever find out about you staying there all that time they were away?"

185

"Well, her mother did, actually. But she took it pretty well." He grinned. "She thinks I'm such a responsible, trustworthy guy that—"

"Yeah, wait till she finds out."

"No, the point is, she knows that Tess and I, you know . . ."

"How does she know?"

"Well, this past year, we used to write letters, kind of . . . well, referring to . . . and her mother found one."

"Oh." I hoped I didn't look funny. I smiled at him. "So, I guess you'll have a good senior year," I said.

He laughed and ruffled my hair. "I guess I will. Look after Mom, okay?"

I nodded. "You were right," I said after a second.

"About what?"

"About Mom and Peggy, you know—how they feel about each other."

"Oh yeah, right . . . well, it's just one of those things."

I hate it when Martin does that, just brushing everything off. "But what do you really think?"

He looked at me thoughtfully. "I really think it's none of my damn business *what* they do, as long as I don't have to watch."

"That's *all* you think?"

"Ali, listen, it's their life, right? They chose that because it made sense to them."

"It doesn't seem weird to you at all?"

"No. Look, she tried the other thing and it didn't work out. Maybe this won't work out either. You just never know."

I hate it when people say things like that. I hate thinking of everything being so insecure. "Don't you think they'll be happy together?"

"How can I tell? They seem to get along. How do I know what'll happen with me and Tess? You just go with it, and you hope for the best."

"Sure." I twisted my hair around my finger, frowning.

"Don't worry so much about it, Ali. They have their life, you have yours. So, live it. And let them worry about living theirs."

"Okay," I said. "I will."

He hugged me and walked off, waving.

At around noon Eileen came back. I guess she'd been at her office. "Are your reservations all set?" she asked brightly.

"Yes, we got a two o'clock flight," Mom said.

"I wish I could drive you," she said, "but I have a patient who would be hard to rearrange."

"That's okay," Mom said. "We'll manage."

"We're going to miss Ali," Eileen said. "It's been lovely having her here."

"I'm sure she'll miss you too," Mom said. She looked at me meaningfully. "Won't you Ali?"

"Oh yeah," I said quickly. "A lot. Well, I'll be back next summer."

"Time always flies in the winter," Eileen said.

Mom went inside. I helped Eileen put the stuff away in the kitchen.

"Well, I'm glad we all . . . I'm glad things have worked out," Eileen said.

"Me too."

"Harold wanted . . . it's hard for him only seeing you two months a year," she went on. "And then, well, his family background *is* rather conservative. He never . . . though studies have been done which show that children raised in . . . nonconforming homes . . . often do just as well as other children."

I guess she meant about Mom and Peggy being gay.

"Well! I better get ready for my patient."

She hesitated. "And if you ever, if you have any change of heart, please remember we always . . . we love having you around. You're like a breath of fresh air!"

"I'll remember," I said. I wonder why Eileen talks that way. It's almost like she was in a play.

"Take care!" She waved as she walked away.

Mom came in, struggling with a bag. "So," she said, smiling. "I might as well call a cab."

"Mom?"

"Yeah?"

"Would it be okay if I called Gretchen first, just to say good-bye?"

"Of course, there's no rush."

My heart was beating fast when I dialed. I guess I didn't realize till that second that I wasn't going to see

Gretchen or Ethan again, maybe for a whole *year*. Gretchen answered the phone.

"Gretch? Hi, it's me," I said softly.

"Oh . . . hi," she said, not in such a friendly way, but not the opposite either.

"I'm about to leave for the airport," I said.

"What for?"

"I'm going home."

"To New York?"

"Yeah, with Mom. She came out to get me."

"Oh."

"So, I just thought if you'd like to, you know, write or something, maybe we still could."

There was a pause.

"I need you for my friend," I said. "I really do, Gretch."

"I need you too," Gretchen said softly. "Listen, Ethan's not here. He went out or something."

I felt really disappointed. "Would you tell him I called to say good-bye?"

"Sure."

"So, have a good year and all."

"You too."

But when I hung up, I still felt funny. It was like things were different between us. I wondered if they'd ever be the same again.

I didn't say much on the way to the airport.

"What are you thinking about, hon?" Mom asked after a while.

"Oh, just different things." I looked at her. "Mom, there was this man on the plane coming here—Mr. Peterson. He said he'd call me, and we could go bowling with his daughter, Barbara, but he never did. Martin said I shouldn't have given him Daddy and Eileen's phone number. He thought he was trying to pick me up or something. Isn't that ridiculous?"

"Well," Mom said carefully. "It's true that on the whole, perhaps it's wise to be a little careful."

"He was *married!* He was, like, forty years old!"

"Well . . . how did your call to Gretchen go?"

I leaned against her. "Okay, I guess. But Ethan wasn't there and I wanted so much to say good-bye to him." I sighed. "I think maybe I'm in love with him."

Mom smiled.

"Are you worried that I'm too young?"

"*I* was in love at fifteen."

"Who with?"

"Oh, his name was Michael. He lived in our apartment building, and I used to meet him in the elevator when I walked our dog. He had a dog too, a St. Bernard, and we had this dachshund that always used to bark at big dogs. I used to feel so ashamed because Peter, our dachshund, would lunge at this poor, polite St. Bernard that was just standing there, minding his own business."

"So what happened?" I asked, really curious.

"Nothing, really. That was all. I think his family moved away while I was in high school."

"You mean, you never even went *out* or anything?"

She shook her head.

That didn't sound like love to *me*. "That sounds more like you just had a crush on him," I said. "That doesn't sound like real *love*."

"No, you're right," she said. "It *wasn't* real love. Is it real love with you and Ethan?"

"Yes," I said, but that's all I said. I didn't feel like talking about it. I was scared she'd ask me if we'd done it or if I knew about birth control and stuff like that. I hate conversations like that. I wish mothers just assumed you knew all that stuff.

Peggy met us at the airport. She hugged both of us. "Hey, look at that tan! You look terrific, Ali."

"Thanks. You look nice too."

"You know, there's one weird thing about me," Peggy said as we walked to the check-out place.

"Only one?" Mom said teasingly.

"No, I mean I just don't tan."

"Do you burn?" I asked.

"I don't do anything! It's strange. I lie in the sun for hours, and I stay the same damn color. Listen, I think I found us a great place."

"Where?" Mom asked.

"A hundred and third and Riverside. But we've got to go right over there, like tonight maybe, because some other couple is interested, and I had to do a lot of fast talking to get the guy to hold it for us."

"Isn't that a little far uptown?" Mom said. "I mean, that neighborhood—"

"Cyn, I lived there," Peggy said.

"You did?" Mom said. "When?"

"Oh, years ago, when I was a mere slip of a girl. I used to walk my dog in Riverside Park all the time and nothing terrible ever happened."

"What kind of dog?" I asked.

"A cocker spaniel. . . . Hey, I have an idea. Why don't we go straight from here up to the apartment? If those people beat us to the punch, I'll be so mad. There's a great view and three bedrooms. What do you say, Ali?"

"Sure, I don't mind."

Peggy dashed off to get a cab. Mom looked at me and grinned. "Welcome to real life," she said.

I wasn't sure if she meant New York, the traffic, the weather, her and Peggy, school starting again, or what. But before I had a chance to say anything, Peggy dragged us into the cab and we set off to look at the new apartment.

Seventeen

We did end up taking that apartment. It's nice, way up on the fourteenth floor so there's lots of sun, especially in the living room and Mom and Peggy's bedroom. That's good for Peggy because she likes plants. The third bedroom is kind of like a den or a study. The TV is in there, and Mom has a desk so she can work late at night if she has to.

The odd thing is, nothing seems very different. I thought now that I know about Mom and Peggy, I would notice things I hadn't before, but I don't. Mostly, they just joke around and act like good friends. They still don't call each other "darling" or kiss a lot. I don't know if that's because they think it would make me uncomfortable or what. I haven't talked about it with anyone at school. One day I brought Amanda home. She's a new girl at my school that I like a lot. I just told her my parents are divorced and my brother lives in California with my father. I was showing her the apartment, and when I came to Mom and Peggy's room, I said, sort of casually, "That's Mom and Peggy's room."

"Who's Peggy?"

"She's my mother's friend. She lives with us."

Amanda didn't ask anything more about it. I think maybe when I know her better, I might tell her about it, but not right now.

During the second week of school something happened that made me feel good, though it was awkward in some ways. We were studying President Roosevelt, and a girl in our class said she'd read this article that said how maybe Mrs. Roosevelt had been gay—how she'd written all these letters to this woman and said stuff about kissing her. Then, this other girl, Marjorie Donally, got up and said she thought it was disgusting to say something like that about Mrs. Roosevelt—because she was a great American.

"And you feel those two things are incompatible?" our teacher, Mr. Lewis, said. He has this flat, quiet voice, so it's hard to tell what side he's on. "You don't think someone can be gay *and* be a great American?"

"I just think it's a dirty rumor," Marjorie said, turning red. "Just like they used to say President Roosevelt was a Communist. They just want to make people think she was weird."

Then this boy named Allen Russo, who has a kind of crush on me and is sort of a hulk—I think he was left back in the fifth grade—said, "Well, it *is* weird for two women to be writing about kissing each other! It sounds pretty weird to *me*."

194

"Well, *you* ought to know, as far as being weird goes," Marjorie snapped.

There was this long discussion that took up almost the whole session—about famous people who were gay and stuff like that. At the very end, this extremely quiet girl named Janet Markowitz, who hardly ever talks in class, raised her hand. "I just wanted to say my brother's gay," she said, "and he's the smartest, nicest person in the world. He knows more about history and music than *anyone*, and if any of you met him, you'd see he isn't one *bit* weird." She glared at everyone as though daring them to say something.

The bell had rung, so Mr. Lewis just ended by saying how people were all different and we should respect individual differences because that was what made life interesting.

After class I went over to Janet. "I think I agree with you," I said, "and I think your brother sounds like a very nice person."

"*I'm* a very nice person," Allen said, going past us.

"Will you bug off, Allen?" Janet said. "Boy, is he a creep!"

"Yeah, well." I walked away, feeling I hadn't said what I wanted to exactly. It's hard to know how to say things.

The first week after school started I wrote a letter to Gretchen and Ethan. I decided to write to them together because writing them separately seemed awkward. Gretchen answered first. Here's what she wrote:

Sept. 20, 1980

Dear Ali,

I meant to write to you before, but I've been really busy with school and dancing and all. My teacher put me in a really advanced class. I'm glad, only it means a lot of work. I might even have to start appearing in productions. Mom is kicking up a big fuss, saying I can only do it if I can keep my schoolwork up too. But the thing is, I care a lot more about dancing than school. I don't even know if I want to *go* to college, but I won't tell her that now.

I've been thinking a lot about everything that happened—about you and Ethan liking each other. It hurts in a way. It still does, and maybe it always will. I don't like to think of myself as a jealous person, but I must be. I think it's that I don't make friends all that easily, so the ones I have matter, maybe more than they should. I guess I want you both all to myself. But I'm trying to fight that. I don't think you meant to hurt me, either of you, so I just have to try and get over it! I thought of what you said on the phone, that you needed me for a friend. I need you too. The point is, Ethan's going off to college, and things with him wouldn't be the same anyway, the same as they were. He just won't *be* there! And neither will you. I'll have to learn to cope and handle things, and just know that you're both out there, caring for me, but not there to hold my hand every second if something goes wrong.

One sad thing happened. It may seem selfish of me not to mention it till the end—Mom lost her baby. I gather it's rare to lose it that far along—she was in her fifth month, and she was pretty hysterical about it for a while. But now—this is hard to believe—she's going around saying this was a "sign" that her baby days are over. I really have the feeling that deep down everyone, including Roger, is a little relieved. I mean, let's face it, being a mother is not exactly her strong point. I've tried to refrain from pointing that out!

So, how are things back home? Is it peaceful not having Martin around? No more dirty letters to peek at! I saw him a couple of times at school. I hate to say this, but he is *so* good-looking! He and Tess still seem to be pretty heavy together, hand in hand, all that.

Write, okay? Let me know how things are. I miss you!

Love,
G.

I felt so good after I read Gretchen's letter. It's true, I like Amanda and some other friends at school but not in the same way. I feel like it's special with Gretchen because we've been friends so long. I mean, she knew me when I was four-feet tall and when I had a crush on Danny Goldberg in fourth grade. And we've been through so many dumb things together, trick or treating the time that weird man asked us to come back for a drink, and the time I set her hair on fire by mistake when we were putting candles out for Christmas. It's just different, having shared so many things. I wrote her back right away. I told her the whole thing about Mom and Peggy.

What's odd is that Ethan didn't write me at all! Maybe he thought Gretchen would be jealous. But then, a month later, I got a letter from him. He wrote:

Oct. 16, 1980

Dear Ali,

I guess Gretchen wrote you all our news, so I'm just writing to say I'll be in New York in two weeks to have my Columbia interview. I thought maybe we could get together, if you'd like to. I'll save whatever else I have to say for then.

Love,
Ethan

Boys are really strange! He thought we could get together "if I'd like to?" Does he really think I *wouldn't* like to? You'd never know from his letter that we'd talked about so many personal things, that we'd lain in each other's arms, kissing, saying we loved each other. I hope *so* much it doesn't mean his feelings about me are different. Looking back on it, I feel like maybe I did kind of throw myself at him a little. It would be awful if he's thought it over and decided I'm not his type. I pray that's not why his letter was so cut and dried.

I wrote him right back and said he could come for dinner and even stay over with us if he wanted, so he wouldn't have to pay for a hotel. That night at dinner I asked Mom about it before I mailed the letter.

"Mom, the thing is, Ethan's coming to New York in a few weeks for his college interview. So I thought, well . . . would you mind if he stayed over for one night?"

"It's fine with me," Mom said, reaching for the coffee pot.

"Who's Ethan?" Peggy asked.

"He's this friend of mine from Berkeley," I said, blushing. "He's my best friend Gretchen's brother."

"Oh yeah," Peggy said. "I remember."

I guess Mom must have mentioned I liked him.

"I didn't know he was thinking of Columbia," Mom said.

I don't think she meant that in any meaningful way, like he was applying there so he could see me more, but I felt funny. "He wants a place with a good science department," I said. "That's what he's interested in."

"Which science?" Peggy asked.

"I think geology," I said.

"I was a geology major in college," Peggy said.

"You were?" said Mom, surprised.

"Yeah, it was strange. I was lousy at science on the whole, but I had this great teacher and I got totally swept up in rock formations and how the earth was formed and all that. And then, all of a sudden my senior year, I thought: ye Gods, I don't want to be a geologist."

"Huh," Mom said, smiling at her. "Will wonders never cease."

"Probably not," Peggy said, smiling back.

At times like that, you can tell they really like each other.

I was so excited the day Ethan was coming for dinner that I hardly listened to *anything* at school. I didn't want to look *too* dressed up when he came, but I wanted to wear something special. Finally I decided to wear these new red corduroy jeans I got this fall and a red and white checked shirt. My hair is a little bit different than it was over the summer. I had it cut with wings on the sides and it's a little shorter, more up to my shoulders. I brought a photo of Cheryl Tiegs—sometimes people say I look like her—and asked the hairdresser to cut it that way. Hairdressers never like it when you ask them to copy somebody else's hair style, but it turned out pretty well. Everyone at school says I look really cute. I have new lip glosses, too, that come in different fruit scents. I wore the one called Strawberry Pink. I think more people like strawberries than grapes or pineapples.

Ethan looked all dressed up too when he came, I guess because of the interview. He was wearing a jacket and a tie. He looked nice. I kissed him quickly and took him into the apartment.

Peggy was in the kitchen fixing dinner. She gets home before Mom on Tuesdays, so she usually fixes dinner then. "Peggy, this is Ethan," I said.

Peggy was just putting the chicken in the oven. "Hi, Ethan, I hope you like chicken."

"Sure," Ethan said. He seemed a little shy.

At dinner Mom asked him how the interview had gone.

Ethan made a face. "Well, I think it was okay," he said slowly, "only at one point the interviewer asked me what my hobbies were, and I said listening to classical music. Then he asked me what the last concert I'd been to was, and I just couldn't remember. My mind went completely blank. And then the second I walked out the door, I remembered the whole program!"

Peggy reached over and took another piece of chicken. "God, I *totally* screwed up my Radcliffe interview. I was so eager to impress the woman with my worldly knowledge that when she asked what my favorite book was, I said *Lady Chatterly's Lover*. I remember her eyes kind of widened and she said, 'Yes, he's such an imaginative stylist, isn't he?' " She laughed.

"I was a mess because of my math scores," Mom said. "They were in the four hundreds. I just guessed at random."

"Why?" Ethan asked, buttering a roll.

"I just panicked. I had such good grades in math, too."

"It's funny," Peggy said, "how little difference it makes twenty years later. I thought I'd die if I didn't get into Radcliffe, and here I am, alive and kicking."

"True," Mom said, smiling. "The wisdom of middle age."

Peggy made a face at her. "Slow down, kid! I'm not ready for middle age, yet."

"Who is?" Mom said, getting up to clear the table.

Usually after dinner, Mom and Peggy work or read or, if there's something good on TV, we might watch it in the den. Peggy goes to bed at ten every night. Sometimes Mom stays up late working in the den. But this night, they both went in at ten.

"Show Ethan where the extra blankets are, Ali, okay?" Mom said.

The den has a studio couch. You just take off the cover and make it up like a regular bed. I brought in the sheets and Ethan and I made it up together. Then I got out this really nice down comforter that belongs to Peggy.

"It has real feathers," I said.

Ethan ran his hand over it. "It looks really warm," he said.

Then we just stood there and looked at each other. It was sort of awkward. "You can use the bathroom in my room," I said, "if you want to take a shower or something."

"Okay." Ethan took his pajamas and toothbrush out of his bag and went into the bathroom. I heard the water running, so I knew he was taking a shower. I'd taken a shower and washed my hair after I'd gotten home from school. So I wasn't sure what to do now—if I should change into my nightgown or what. I just sat on the edge of the bed.

When Ethan came out of the bathroom, he had put on his clothes again. That seemed odd, because he'd brought his pajamas into the bathroom. He came over to where I was sitting. "Well, I'll see you in the morning," he said, and he leaned over and kissed me on the cheek. Then he went back into the den.

I couldn't *believe* it! I felt so awful. I don't think I've ever felt so bad in my whole life. I mean, here we hadn't seen each other for two months and all he does is kiss me on the cheek! He must have a girlfriend, and I guess he didn't want to tell me.

I put on my nightgown and got into bed. But I couldn't fall asleep. I just lay there, looking at the ceiling. I felt so bad I couldn't even cry. I felt like biting my hand or punching the wall as hard as I could. It was like there was a pain in my stomach—a horrible, hard knot and I could hardly even swallow.

Then suddenly I decided to go in and ask Ethan if he has a girlfriend. I mean, I'd rather know. If he does, then that's okay. Why shouldn't he?

I opened my door and just as I started down the hall, I bumped into Ethan. We looked at each other, surprised.

"I just thought . . ." he started.

"There's something I want to ask you," I said grimly.

"Should we go in my room or yours?"

"Yours." I went in and sat down on the edge of the bed. "Do you have a girlfriend?" I asked, making myself look right at him.

Ethan smiled. "Only you," he said, sort of sheepishly.

I frowned. "So, how come you just kissed me on the cheek?"

"Cowardice." After a second he said, "Do you want to get in bed a minute?"

"Okay." I snuggled in under the comforter. I was glad I'd worn my new nightgown. It's light blue, baby doll style, and has bikini underpants to match. "Don't you like the comforter?" I said. "It's so nice and fluffy."

"I love it," Ethan said, and he pulled me into his arms. "I'm sorry about before," he said in a low voice.

"That's okay," I said. "I just got scared . . . that maybe you didn't feel the same way as you did over the summer."

He was silent a moment. "I think it's that I felt a little awkward with your mother and Peggy."

"You mean about their being gay?"

"Not about it so much. But I couldn't help feeling they might not like men in general that much and might feel critical of anyone you bring home. It's just my feeling. I'm not saying it's true. Really, they were very friendly."

"They're not like that," I said. But I understood how he felt. "Mom thinks you're very nice."

"Yeah, well, I guess it was just something I worried about." He hesitated. "And I wasn't sure . . . well, the way you wrote to Gretchen and me together. I thought maybe once you got back home, the whole thing seemed . . . too complicated and you wanted to just go back to the way it was before."

"No!" I said. "Not at all. I just couldn't figure out how to handle it. I didn't want to hurt Gretchen."

"So it was just that?"

"Sure."

"You still feel—"

"Yes," I said before he could even finish. I looked up at him. "I think about you all the time."

He smiled. "I think about you a lot too."

"I'm glad. . . ." I took a deep breath. "Kiss me!"

"I think that can be arranged," Ethan said.

We started kissing and pretty soon we took off our clothes. My heart was beating as fast as if I'd been running in a marathon. Ethan ran his hands down my body; his mouth was open and wet against my neck.

"Ethan?"

"What?"

"I want to do it now."

"Okay," Ethan said.

"Do you have any, you know, stuff for birth control or something? I don't."

"Yeah, I have something," he said, sort of embarrassed. He went and got a package from his coat pocket. "I hope these are okay," he said, taking out some condoms.

"Why shouldn't they be?" I asked nervously.

"Well, they're sort of old."

"How old?"

He smiled sheepishly. "I got them three years ago."

Three years! "Don't they keep? What happens to them if they get old?"

"I don't know." He looked at it. "It *looks* okay."

I was nervous anyway. "What if it rips in the middle?"

"It won't," he said, putting it on. "This is a good quality kind. I read the wrapper."

"Oh . . . does it feel funny?" I looked at it. It looked like rubber cement had been poured on his penis.

"A little."

"How come you've been carrying it around for three years?"

"I haven't been carrying it *around* exactly. I just had it in my drawer, waiting for the right moment."

We began kissing again. I felt nervous. "I feel funny," I whispered, "with Peggy and Mom right in the next room."

"We don't *have* to do it," Ethan said softly.

"Yes, we do."

"We do?"

I laughed nervously. "No, seriously, I want to. I just feel nervous, that's all."

"Me too."

"It's not supposed to be that good the first time, so don't expect too much," I said.

"Oh, I'm not," Ethan said. "I'm just going to grit my teeth and wait for it to be over."

I hugged him. "I love you."

"I love you too, Ali."

And then we did it. I remember this girl in my school who finally did it with her boyfriend saying, "It's not such a big deal." All of us felt so disappointed, afraid it was another thing that gets built up, and then is nothing like what you expect. It did hurt with Ethan, especially in the beginning, but it was exciting anyway. I kept thinking, "Now we really belong to each other." In a funny way it didn't hurt so much then.

Afterward we lay in each other's arms, feeling so nice and warm. I decided not to tell Ethan it had hurt at all. I was afraid that might make him feel bad. It wasn't his fault. I guess that's just the way it is, in the beginning at least. One thing I'm glad of. I'm really glad I waited to do it with someone I really love who really loves me. Maybe it would be good the other way, but this way it was special.

I stayed in bed with Ethan all night, but at about four I went back to my room so Mom and Peggy wouldn't notice anything when they got up. I didn't really go back to sleep. I just lay there, thinking about everything, and feeling good and wishing Ethan didn't have to go away.

I have to leave for school at eight so it was sort of rushed in the morning. I tried not to look at Ethan too much because I was afraid Mom or Peggy might notice something. But I did go into his room to say good-bye.

We said how much we'd miss each other.

"I hope you get into Columbia," I said. I started to cry, even though I'd told myself I wouldn't.

Ethan hugged me close. "I will, Ali, don't worry. I'll get in."

It'll be hard being apart all year. I almost wish I had stayed out in Berkeley. But then Mom might have thought I didn't approve of her and Peggy, and I wouldn't want her to feel that way. There are just different ways of loving people, that's all; there's no one right way. I guess you have to sort of figure it out as you go along.

When I got home, Mom was there. She said, "Oh hi, Ali Cat . . . . How was school?"

"Mom, I don't think you should call me that anymore. It's sort of a baby name, you know?"

Mom looked at me thoughtfully for a moment. "It's true," she said. "You're not a baby anymore, are you?"

"No," I said. "I'm not."

NORMA KLEIN, one of the most popular writers for young people today, grew up in New York City. She received a B.A. from Barnard College and an M.A. from Columbia University. Ms. Klein is the author of four adult novels, numerous books for children and teenagers, and over sixty short stories. Her best known books for young people include *Love Is One of the Choices, Mom, the Wolf Man and Me, Confessions of an Only Child* and *A Honey of a Chimp* (the latter three published by Pantheon).

Ms. Klein is currently a contributing editor of *Working Mother*. She and her husband, Erwin Fleissner, live with their two daughters on Manhattan's Upper West Side.